'I'm just trying to figure you out and——' Jake shrugged, and he looked strangely at a loss for words.

'Why?' Jenny asked with a tinge of desperation in her voice. 'Why do you have to figure me out?'

He shook his head, his hands moving along her arms, palms brushing her skin. 'I don't know,' he admitted, drawing her closer, kissing her with a sudden, rough gentleness, not giving her time to respond or push away before his hands dropped and she was standing alone, staring at him, finding herself aching for his touch.

'Jake,' she whispered. 'Please don't——'

He waited for her to finish, but she shrugged and turned away. 'Goodnight, Jake.'

He didn't try to stop her, but his deep voice followed her. 'Jennifer Winslow, you intrigue the hell out of me.'

JENNY'S TURN

BY

VANESSA GRANT

MILLS & BOON LIMITED
ETON HOUSE   18-24 PARADISE ROAD
RICHMOND   SURREY   TW9 1SR

First published in Great Britain 1987
by Mills & Boon Limited

© Vanessa Grant 1987

Australian copyright 1987
Philippine copyright 1988
This edition 1988

ISBN 0 263 75868 0

Set in Times Roman 10 on 11 pt.
01-0188-56434 C

Printed and bound in Great Britain by
Collins, Glasgow

This book is dedicated to my mother
and, of course, to Brian

CHAPTER ONE

JENNY was editing a videotape, trying to ignore interruptions. Charlotte, at the switchboard, knew that she was out to all callers—except, of course, to Jake.

Charlotte was new, not long out of business school. Given time, Jenny hoped she would turn into an efficient receptionist. Today, she was simply hoping that Charlotte had the tact and sense to keep any callers happy while keeping them away from Jenny.

Normally she could work intensely for hours, shutting out the noises around her, tuning into her work. Not on this job.

Last month, she had asked Jake to give her a challenge, a new project to work on. He'd handed her the Madison contract.

Hamburgers!

How could *anyone* get excited about doing training films for a fast-food chain? There! The grand finale! The hot, steaming beef patty resting on a bun dripping with relish—— Darn! She could have sworn she had already cut out that shot. The refuse bin showed all too clearly in the background!

A door slammed, echoing through the building.

Jenny's hand jerked, sending a sharp black line through her notes. Her heart thudded a crashing impact against her ribcage.

Jake!

Other people opened that door gently. Jake always burst in, throwing it open explosively. Once, she had suggested that he have a rubber stopper installed, but he'd shrugged and laughed. She suspected he never

7

noticed the noise it made. Or did he notice, and like the effect?

'Any messages, Charlotte?' His voice was like the rest of him. Too big, too aggressive. It carried clearly from the outer office. No one ignored Jake. Jenny tried, looking back down at the Madison hamburger.

'Jennifer?' he called out, before he even got to her doorway. How could anyone ignore that voice?

He expected her to drop whatever she was doing and dash out to see what he wanted. She was used to that. Normally, it wouldn't bother her, but lately——

She let her long, brown hair fall across her face as she concentrated on the film. If she let him interrupt her now, she'd have to watch the whole darned thing again to get the feel for that last scene!

'Jennifer?' He was towering over her table now. She punched the pause button and watched the scene freeze on her monitor.

'How did you make out with the Eglinton film I gave you?' He leaned on to her desk to look at her monitor.

She switched the power off and looked up, trying to tell herself it wasn't his nearness that made her short of breath. He was alive, vital—sexy, she admitted with a frown. The room pulsed with his suppressed energy, the excitement that he brought to everything around him. His face reflected it—not handsome, but dark and aggressive and filled with the sharply drawn lines of his laughter and his frowns.

Life around Jake couldn't help being fascinating. Jenny's work days held a lot more excitement than her leisure, although she had been left behind more and more this last year, even since Jake had hired Hans as a photographer.

Until then, it had been Jenny who followed Jake on location. Then everything had changed. Jenny had seriously considered quitting when she discovered that

Hans was taking her place on location—at Jake's request!

She didn't really know why she had stayed, outwardly accepting her new role, but resenting it terribly every time Jake walked out the door with Hans trailing behind him.

Sometimes she had the urge to scream at him, but Jake wasn't the kind of person you went up against and won.

Right now, standing over her desk, he was determined to discuss Eglinton, and couldn't care less that he was messing up her concentration on the Hamburger Caper.

Monica never saw this side of him, the maddening, aggravating Jake Austin. Poor Monica, she had no idea what she was getting into—dating this man with the harsh, predatory face.

He was tall and dark, lean and hard, pulsing with the suppressed energy that had made Austin Media one of the most successful documentary film companies on Canada's West Coast. And he had been dating Jenny's room-mate for six months, ever since the day Jenny's car had broken down and he had given her a ride home.

With his usual lack of restraint, he'd been questioning Jenny about Wayne, her latest boyfriend. He was always asking about the men she dated. Jenny usually concentrated on hiding her resentment at his questions, using whatever tactic was handy to avoid answering.

This time she had used Monica. She'd known her room-mate was home, and had invited Jake in for coffee as much to distract him as anything else.

Monica had been reading a book when they came in. Jenny had introduced them, glancing at Jake, then back to Monica, feeling herself suddenly outside, looking in on the beginnings of Jake's next affair.

Now, six months later, he was prowling across to his own desk. He stared back at her intently, as if he'd been reading her thoughts. 'About the film?' he reminded her, ejecting a video cartridge from his camera as he watched her.

'I took it home last night,' she conceded.

'And——?' He swung back to her table. She had once believed that brown eyes were warm and soft. His were sometimes hot, sometimes cold, but seldom soft. Right now they penetrated, trying to see everything. She fiddled with the controls on the tape player, uncomfortably aware of the way her suit jacket had fallen back to reveal the swell of her breasts through her blouse.

After five years she should have grown used to the way his eyes would suddenly lock on her body, taking in every detail, noticing as she uneasily adjusted her jacket.

'The film,' she repeated. 'Yes, I think it would make a good documentary.'

'You can write the script,' he offered casually.

'On location?' she asked, her eyes sparkling with sudden anticipation.

His dark eyes met hers for an uncomfortable moment, then he was back at his own desk on the far side of the room, sorting through papers. 'There's no need for you to go on location. You'll have the videotape, the sound-tracks.' She made her face into a mask, hiding her disappointment at his explanation. '...need you here. I talked to Chris Eglinton this morning—his plans, some of his ideas. I got it on tape. See him yourself. Get a feel for what he's doing, then rough in a story-board for me— I'd like it by tomorrow.'

His fingers brushed hers as she took the tape. She frowned, ignoring the tingle from his touch. She clenched the tape tightly, hiding the sudden anger she couldn't help feeling, protesting, 'I can't do it, Jake, not for tomorrow. I've got the Madison film to finish, and I can't stay late tonight. I'm going out with Wayne.'

'Put him off—he'll forgive you. Please, Jennifer?'

Jennifer. He was the only one that used that name. It reminded her of Lance. She hated the reminder, yet it kept her safe from any temptation to let herself be caught up in Jake's web of romance.

'Jenny?' Charlotte called through from the next room. 'Call for you—or—you said not to interrupt you?'

Jake snorted and rolled his eyes in exasperation. Jenny shrugged, smiling herself. Charlotte's inefficiencies were becoming a daily joke they shared.

'Take a message, Charlotte!' she called, wondering if Charlotte would ever learn to use the intercom.

Jake said, 'No, take the call.'

'Give her time,' Jenny said quietly to him. 'She's young.' But she resisted his smile, remembering that she was angry at him. Would she *ever* get to go on location again? Would it always be Hans, usurping her place? Jake was watching, seeing too much. Jenny picked up the telephone, saying casually, 'Jenny Winslow here.'

'George Dobson here. I thought I'd find you at this number. Still working for your Haida chieftain?'

'My——' She looked up at Jake, met his eyes, dark above prominent cheekbones. She glanced quickly away from their probing examination. Was that anger, or— Could he hear George's voice? She hoped not. '*George*, where are you? I haven't heard from you in so long! Are you——'

Jake turned away impatiently. Jenny forced her fingers to relax on the receiver as George said, 'Slow down, darling! I'm in Alaska, just flying out. I'll be in Vancouver tomorrow.'

'Really? Tomorrow?' Jake was watching her again, but she couldn't stop an excited, 'I can hardly wait! Do you *realise* how long it's been?' She saw so little of her family, and George was the closest of them all.

'I know. I had to be off on my own, Jenny. I know I neglected you. I'll be there tomorrow and you can chastise me properly. You will have dinner with me tomorrow, won't you?'

'Of course I will.' She laughed happily, then sobered, asking, 'You did say Alaska?'

'I'll explain tomorrow. I'll call you at work.'

Jenny was left staring at a dead telephone receiver. 'George, damn you!' she muttered, but she couldn't help smiling. George hadn't changed since they were children. Always doing the unexpected, never explaining until she was ready.

'George?' Jake was demanding 'Who the hell is George?'

She put the phone down slowly, registering Jake's fierce expression, smothering a smile. George was wrong in calling him a chief, but it wasn't hard to picture him in the traditional clothes of his Haida ancestors. 'What did you say?' she asked, playing for time to assess his mood.

'George, you said.' He was talking slowly, as if to a child. 'Are you two-timing Wayne? You have a date with Wayne tonight. Or had you forgotten?'

'You should know,' she said, keeping her voice carefully neutral. 'You keep better track of my social life than I do. Are you doing a documentary on me? I doubt if there's a market for it.'

He frowned darkly, turning away, throwing back, 'Don't forget that story-board.'

She didn't know whether to laugh or to throw something after him as he left. Then she did laugh, thinking of George—small and blonde and very female. George certainly wasn't any competition for Wayne!

Jake must have heard her chuckle. He made a sudden, angry gesture to Hans. The photographer scurried to gather his camera and recorder, tearing out the door before it slammed closed.

They all jumped when Jake commanded. Arrogant, temperamental man! Some day, she'd like to give him a piece of her mind.

She called Wayne before going back to work.

'About tonight——' she began.

'Don't, Jenny! Don't cancel on me tonight! Tonight's special,' he protested.

'I'm not,' she denied, mentally rearranging her evening. 'I have to go to the library. Some research I have to do. Could you pick me up there? About seven?'

It wasn't the way she'd planned the night. She'd intended to ask Jake if she could leave early. She'd wanted to spend an hour in the sauna at a nearby health spa, getting rid of every trace of the working girl.

Wayne was nothing like Jake. Jake's attraction was dark and dangerous. He always stirred her emotions—sometimes excitement, sometimes anger. She had a hot temper, well concealed, but she knew better than to let herself lose control around Jake. He was always watching, waiting for some clue to her that would give him an advantage.

Jake thought she had a heavy romance going with Wayne. He was wrong. They were no more than friends. They'd been dating for several months, ever since Wayne had turned up at her door one day, looking sheepish and a little ill at ease.

'I've just come from the Caribbean.' He'd introduced himself quickly, as if he were afraid she would slam the door in his face. 'I was teaching at the technical institute there—I worked with your father.'

She'd opened the door wide, welcoming him. Her mother's monthly duty letters had dwindled since Jenny had left school. Even this second-hand contact was something to grasp at, to give her a feeling of family.

That had been the beginning, and they'd seen each other regularly since. Much of Jenny's time was spent listening to his problems finding a job, but tonight would be different. Wayne was celebrating getting a two-year contract for a teaching job in Saudi Arabia, and Jenny didn't want to let him down by cancelling at the last minute.

Wayne was the kind of boyfriend that suited her: friendly but not too amorous. She didn't want a lover, or a husband. She'd seen enough disasters. George, for one, although George had been in love with Scott—but look at her now: alone and rattling around the world in a desperate search for something.

That wasn't for Jenny. Wayne was leaving, but she had holidays coming, and she wasn't planning to get miserable about saying goodbye.

She thought about her holidays as she was working her way through Eglinton's thickest book in the library. She'd made reservations for a flight to the Caribbean to visit her parents. They had got into the habit of taking holidays in Fiji since she'd left university, so she hadn't seen them in several years.

She'd phone them with her arrival time, get on the plane—too bad there wasn't time to go by bus or boat, anything but flying!—then she'd arrive at the airport, be met——

All right, be a realist, Jenny. Her parents wouldn't meet her at the airport. She would take a taxi, or whatever the local equivalent was. She'd arrive and her mother would give her a cool kiss. Her father would look at her with that vague, troubled gaze, as if he wasn't sure where she'd come from.

She frowned at the library book in her hands, concentrating until she tuned out her parents. When Wayne came, she was still surrounded by books and papers, but she packed everything up quickly, determined to enjoy her evening.

After dinner Wayne drove to Spanish Banks, parking the car where they could look out over the ocean. The moon was hanging over English Bay. Jenny snuggled down in the curve of Wayne's arm, comfortably watching the reflections on the water.

When he kissed her, she let her lips soften against his, enjoying stirrings of warmth. This was just right. Pleasant, but no threat to her equilibrium. She wasn't going to lose her head. Or her heart. She settled closer into his arms, half opened her eyes and saw the moon hanging over his shoulder.

Parked by the water, the moon shining down on them—it stirred memories of Lance, and with the memories came the agony and the bitterness.

Lance, she thought. No matter how many men there are, it always comes back to Lance. She had a sudden desperate need to get away, to be alone.

Wayne was stroking her long hair, but he drew back when she started shivering.

'You're cold? That jacket's not very warm, is it?' He shifted, started the engine and said, 'I'll take you home and you can get some sleep.'

But she couldn't seem to shake the memory of Lance. She smiled at Wayne, and managed to kiss him goodbye when he dropped her at her car, but all she was seeing was the past.

Pain. Betrayal. Loss. *Damn!* She didn't want to be bitter, but no one was ever going to get close enough to her again to tear her apart! She would follow Jake's example, walk away from each relationship before it became serious, before anyone got a hold on her.

Jake's love-life was as changeable as the films he worked on. Sometimes she suspected that he changed women every time he finished a major project. The brunette had been during the ecology series. The redhead must have been around election time, when Jake had been up to his ears in political broadcasts. And Monica——

Monica had lasted longer than the others.

Why on earth did she feel like crying?

She parked underground and took the elevator up to her apartment, her arms loaded with books and the story-board pad.

The apartment was dark, except for the numbers glowing on a digital clock in the living-room. Monica was out with Jake. She might stay out all night. Of course, they must be lovers. *Monica and Jake.* They'd be at his False Creek town house, her arms twisted around his broad shoulders, his eyes glowing as they looked down on her pale body. The blankets would be tumbled around them, evidence of their passion.

Jenny shivered again. The thermostat said twenty degrees, but it had to be wrong. She turned it up to twenty-five.

She had been at Jake's town house once, for a party. She could close her eyes and see it clearly. She'd stood at the window and looked out over the water, staring at the boats in the marina below. Behind her, Jake had been dancing with his current woman.

Was he dancing with Monica tonight? Or making love?

Jenny moved restlessly, putting a tape in the stereo, pouring herself a Coke and carrying it into her bedroom, where she had a workbench set up.

She tried to keep working when she heard the door, the low sound of Jake's voice, then Monica's. She stared at the words she had written on the story-board, but they made no sense at all. She'd lost her concentration. Their voices kept intruding on her work.

She was hungry, but she'd have to walk past Jake and Monica on her way to the kitchen. Jake would be watching her as if he knew how it bothered her to see them together. She turned out her light and undressed in the glow from a street-lamp. Silence from the living-room. Was Monica kissing him back, her arms twisted around him, her fingers tangling in his black hair? *Why didn't they stay away, do their kissing somewhere else?*

She slipped under the covers of her narrow bed. In the living-room, Jake and Monica certainly weren't making enough noise to keep her awake. Most of the time, they weren't making any noise at all.

She slept, restlessly at first, then deeply. She was lost in some troubled dream when Monica knocked on her bedroom door and called, 'Wake up, sleepy head! You can't sleep for ever.'

Then she was dashing, getting dressed and tending to her hair and teeth. She had time to take a quick gulp of coffee in the kitchen, to listen to Monica saying, 'I'll be away this weekend. Jake's taking me over to Victoria for the weekend. Did you know he has an uncle living over there? Quite an old character, I guess.'

'I might go away for the weekend, too,' lied Jenny as she headed out the door.

She hadn't noticed before, but on the way to work there was a big billboard with a picture of a hamburger on it—a big juicy hamburger with one bite out of it. Jenny could recite, in great and gory detail, the process that had produced that hamburger.

She might *never* eat another hamburger!

CHAPTER TWO

JENNY unloaded the big story-board on to Jake's desk, grabbing quickly to rescue a pile of papers that started to slide off towards the edge of his desk.

'Eglinton?' he asked, looking up, the telephone propped under his chin. She thought he looked strained, tired. She nodded silently and he said, 'There's a message for you on your desk.'

He shifted the receiver, looking as if he were tempted to hang up. How long had he been waiting on hold?

'Jennifer, I wanted to—— Hello? Yes, Jake here. Look, is there any chance of pushing ahead the printing schedule for the museum pamphlets?'

Jenny walked over to her desk, picked up the paper written in Charlotte's round, childish handwriting. 'Dinner at seven. Pick me up at the Holiday Inn. Love, George.'

Then Charlotte was leaning over her shoulder, saying, 'That message came into the answering service before I got here this morning.' She looked at Jenny expectantly, hoping for more information about George than Jenny's brief, 'Thanks.'

George was exactly the therapy she needed. Being around her cousin tended to bring out the rebel in Jenny. When they were children, she and George had always been in scrapes together—going out sailing in Dad's boat without permission, getting caught in the tide rips off Cape Mudge, having a garage sale without asking, starting to sell all Aunt Georgina's treasures from the corners of the attic.

18

Jake was getting up from his desk, prowling restlessly. 'We just *might* get the printers to do the job on time —assuming I can get the copy to them.' He leaned on the edge of her desk, resting on one lean, brown hand. She stared down at his fingers, bare except for a carved silver ring on the baby finger of his left hand.

'You can lock yourself in here and work on it,' she told him, looking up, meeting his eyes with a smile. 'I'll tell Charlotte to give all your calls to me. Leave everything else for a few days.'

He raked his hand through his hair, staring at her lips. She found her smile freezing as he demanded, 'How does this George rate getting you to pick him up? You usually have your men coming for you—— Whatever's happening to Wayne?'

Jake's love-life was probably a darn sight more interesting than Jenny Winslow's—everyone's was—but she made herself keep smiling and said, 'I'm beginning to believe you really *do* want to do a film on my love-life!'

He straightened abruptly, pushing his hand into his pocket. 'You don't give anything away, do you? You're secretive, like an oyster.'

She shrugged and switched the monitor on. 'I like oysters.'

'I *bet* you do—just your style. I don't know any more about you than I did the day you walked into my studio.'

She met his probing eyes defiantly, but kept her voice cool. 'Just what is it that you need to know, Jake?' But he didn't rise to that bait.

He brushed her hair back with his free hand, the glint in his eyes telling her that he knew how hard it was for her not to jerk away.

'The men come and go,' he mused, 'but none of them ever gets near you. All right, keep your secrets. Let's get into the Eglinton thing.'

She relaxed, her fingers dropping George's note into the waste-paper basket. She saw Jake watching the note fall, but he made no comment. Jenny said, 'Eglinton on his mountain-climbing expedition? I think there's a lot of potential.'

And they were off, talking, bouncing ideas back and forth, tearing up the story-board she'd done the night before—she'd known it would suffer that fate. It was only a focal point to get them started, to organise their thoughts.

Maybe this was what kept her working for Jake. The moments when they shared the creation of an idea, when he forgot to watch her and she could relax with the joy of just working with him, until she found herself suggesting eagerly, 'Couldn't I go on location? I'd like a chance to get back into some filming. Since Hans has come, I've been pretty much stuck in the studio.'

'Can't, Jennifer.' His voice was strangely devoid of emotion. 'I need you here. There's too much to do, pulling it all together. On the twentieth——'

Dully, she said, 'I'll be gone, Jake. I'll be on holidays.'

'I meant to talk to you—later. Later today, we'll sit down for a bit and go over a few things.'

But they didn't. Jake left for City Hall to work on an educational film on municipal government. He never did get back to the office. Jenny stayed, working until her watch told her it was six o'clock. Too much work. She would never finish it all in the next week before her holidays—not unless she abandoned the Madison series.

She shook herself impatiently and went for her coat. It was quitting time. Certainly no time to be wondering if she should put off her holidays once again.

Tonight she'd be seeing George for the first time in years. Her cousin had virtually disappeared from sight of her family. She'd sent postcards from France, quick notes from Greece. Jenny had read loneliness between the quickly scrawled words, knowing her cousin was still grieving for Scott.

Yet tonight George seemed as she always had: lively and vivacious, her short blonde hair waving closely around her heart-shaped face, her grin mischievous.

'George, you look gorgeous! You've had your hair streaked—it looks terrific!'

'That's grey hair you see.' George patted the seat beside her. 'Sit down. I'll be thirty soon, getting to be an old lady. Tell me about yourself, Jenny. Men?'

'No one special.' She smiled suddenly, and added, 'Although you'll never convince Jake of that. He thinks I'm the scarlet lady.'

George studied her, frowning. 'Speaking of Jake— how's work? Still loving it?'

'I'm not looking for another job,' Jenny evaded.

George's blue eyes widened. 'Do I detect a note of discontent?'

Jenny laughed. 'You would notice, wouldn't you? Maybe I'm restless—I *am* restless.'

'What about your chieftain?'

'Jake's not mine. I wouldn't want him to be!'

Her words echoed around the table. A woman seated behind George twisted curiously to look at them.

George was staring at her, too. Jenny said hurriedly, 'He's not a chieftain, you know. It was his grandfather who was a Haida chief.'

George pushed back the curls that fell over her forehead. The hair promptly bounced back as her hand left it. 'Jenny, you're getting into a rut. It shows in your voice. You should either make a play for your Jake, or get out.'

Jenny pushed her long hair back nervously, not meeting her cousin's eyes. George, as usual, was able to see right through her. Jake had always affected Jenny more than he should, but lately she'd become almost obsessed——*Lord*! These days he couldn't even come through the door without her heart going wild!

She picked up the menu again, and asked, 'What's good here? What did you order?'

'Come to Alaska with me. I'm going sailing.'

Hardly listening, Jenny repeated, 'Sailing? In Alaska?'

'Have the baked salmon,' said George impatiently, taking Jenny's menu and catching the waitress's eye.

'Sailing?' Jenny said again, finally paying attention. 'Whose boat?'

George picked up a spoon, stirring her coffee for the second time. Her voice was slightly unsteady. 'Scott and I were buying a boat, just before he—before he had his heart attack. The boat was in Alaska. I'm going to take it sailing now. Baked salmon,' she told the waitress.

Jenny echoed her order, frowning, remembering how impulsive her cousin could be. This sounded like a madcap scheme from their childhood.

'Are you sure you know what you're doing?' she asked slowly.

'Positive,' George said firmly. 'Scott and I were going to sail her south, but Scott—he—we—I didn't know what to do, so I had the yard haul the boat out again, store it on dry land. Then I tried to forget about it.'

A tall man in a business suit walked past, staring at George as if he might know her. George ignored him.

Jenny asked, 'You didn't sell the boat?'

'No,' George shrugged, and finally met Jenny's eyes. 'And now I want to make the trip.'

'From Alaska? Alone?' The tall man was seated across from them now, still trying to catch George's eye. 'That man seems to know you—no, not there. The one in the brown suit.'

George looked, then quickly looked away. 'He has the room next to mine. I keep running into him, and he keeps trying to start a conversation. I'll sail alone if I have to, but why don't you come with me?' George laughed, the sparkle returning to her eyes as she said, 'Keep me out of trouble, like old times.'

'You've got to be joking! I never kept you out of trouble—you got me *into* trouble is more like it!' She added, regretfully, 'I can't, George.'

'Are you sure?' George wasn't one to take no for an answer. She persisted, 'Think about it. You've been working there for how long?'

'Five years.' Was it *really* that long since she had walked into Jake's chaotic one-man studio? She'd been job-searching, working her way through the yellow pages of the telephone book, working that day on a hunch that anyone who did documentary films might need someone to write scripts. She'd had a brand new creative-writing degree from the University of Victoria, and she'd already worked her way through all the newspapers and radio stations in her search for a job.

She'd climbed three flights of stairs to find Jake's office. She'd gone in through the door as someone else went out, found herself standing in the midst of chaos—papers, sketches, boxes of supplies. And Jake.

'I'm busy,' he'd informed her rudely, dark eyes meeting hers impatiently, a sketching charcoal in his hand. 'What do you want?'

'A job,' she'd told him, knowing this was the place, that she wanted to work for this man. She'd wanted to come closer, see what he was working on. She'd wanted to share the excitement that seemed to emanate from him.

He'd shaken his head, turned back to his easel, saying, 'Try the accountants downstairs. They might need someone.'

'Not nearly as badly as you do,' Jenny had retorted, pointedly looking around at the chaos of his studio.

George's voice intruded on her memories. 'Are you going to spend the rest of your life working for the man?

You could freelance. Go travelling, see something of the world and take pictures with that video camera of yours.' George spread her hands, indicating a world full of possibilities.

Weakening, Jenny said slowly, 'I've got a month's holidays coming. How long will it take you to come down from Alaska?'

'I've no particular schedule.' George was plainly altering her plans to suit Jenny. 'We could be down on Vancouver Island within a month.'

Jenny frowned, tracing a line on her napkin. 'I'm supposed to start my vacation next week. I was thinking of going to visit Mom and Dad.'

'Is Aunt Sally expecting you?'

'Well—no. I hadn't decided yet.' Jenny shifted her chair to avoid meeting the eye of the man in the brown suit. George had made a conquest there, although she didn't seem to care. 'I did book my ticket, but I keep expecting Jake to tell me I can't go.' Her holidays had already been put off several times because of Jake's demands.

'Cancel the ticket. Tell the chieftain you'll quit if he won't let you go.' George waved a hand in a decisive motion. 'Come for a month, then if you decide to stay we can sail south to the Caribbean and see Aunt Sally and Uncle Herb.'

What a holiday! That was what she needed. A new experience, something that didn't have Jake anywhere around.

Later, when she arrived home, she saw Jake's car in her car park. That prepared her for finding him curled up on the living-room sofa with Monica.

Monica's time must be almost up, thought Jenny wryly, because Jake pushed away from her and got to his feet as Jenny slipped her coat off.

'Didn't he bring you home?' he asked, his hands pushed deep into his pockets. 'You haven't got him very well trained yet.'

'I'll work on it.' Jenny turned away from Jake. 'Hi, Monica.'

'The new boyfriend?' speculated Jake from behind her. 'Or is he an old one come back?'

'Who?' Monica asked from the sofa. She looked indecently contented, thoroughly kissed.

Jake said, 'I wanted to talk to you, Jennifer.'

'About George?'

He said, 'No. About your holidays.'

Jenny had known it was coming. She turned away, fitting her coat carefully on to the hanger as he said, 'You'll have to wait until we get the Eglinton film underway, Jennifer. I can't spare you until then.'

'Oh?' She smoothed the coat, turned and walked into the small kitchenette.

Hans had taken ten days off only a month ago, but not Jenny. She'd been waiting years for more than a long weekend, and now she'd have to wait again! What would he do if she just walked out? He couldn't stop her, could he? He could fire her—serve him right if he did. Then he'd find out just how much work she did, just how badly he needed her.

'Jennifer?' His voice followed her, faintly worried. *Good!* Let him worry, he deserved it. She let the door swing, listening to it click shut, closing him outside.

Mercifully, he didn't follow her.

Monica came a moment later. 'Are you making coffee, Jenny? Jake wants coffee.'

'Does he, now?' Monica stared at her sarcastic tone and Jenny said, quietly, 'I'm boiling water for tea. There's just enough for me.'

She'd like to pour the whole kettleful over his head!

Monica started filling the coffee-maker with water. 'What were you and Jake talking about when you came in?'

'Not much. We were talking about work.'

Monica smiled a dreamy smile and said softly, 'I'm going to marry him, Jenny.'

Jenny's heart slammed against her ribs. She had to clear her throat, but her voice was still hoarse. *'Jake asked you to marry him?'*

'Not yet. But he will.' Monica touched her own lips, almost whispering, 'He's on the verge of it. He's been hinting, and I'm going to say yes when he does. I love him, Jenny. There's nobody else like him.' Monica gave her a quick hug, then slipped away to her lover.

No! Jake didn't *marry* his women. He kept them at a distance, played with them, then let them go.

Jenny watched the steam rising from the kettle, an angry pain washing over her as she thought of Jake and Monica—married.

It would get worse later, when they were actually married. Every day, Jake would leave the studio, go home to Monica. Jenny would watch him go, then she would drive home alone.

She had a terrifying, horrible vision of herself going out walking in the night, going all the way to False Creek, looking up into Jake's window...knowing from the darkened windows that they were lying together, their skin touching from shoulders to thighs.

Oh, God! Surely she wouldn't be such a fool as to do that, wandering around the city like a lovesick fool! Even when Lance had abandoned her, she hadn't been *that* insane with love!

Any man who married Monica would end up having a big family. What kind of a father would Jake make? Loving. Stern sometimes. Monica would have to watch him, be sure he didn't become too intensely involved in work to have time for his children. *My God!* Would they ask her to be godmother?

Jenny could picture their children. She blinked back the tears, angrily tore off a paper-towel square from the holder and roughly dabbed at her eyes.

They looked good together: his dark maleness beside her soft, feminine fairness. His dark, suntanned skin against her white fragility. *Their children——*

The kettle was boiling, steam whistling out of the small hole. She turned it off, set it aside, listening to the sounds it made as the water stopped boiling. She had to get out of here, away from them both before the tears really did come. She'd *never* be able to explain tears to Jake.

She stood very still, breathing heavily as if she'd just run a hard race. She took a deep, calming breath, slowly forcing her heartbeat slower. If Jake wanted coffee this time of night, he'd be planning to go back to work when he left Monica. Did Monica realise that?

Monica might have it wrong. Jake wasn't one for hinting. Or marrying.

Jennifer. He *always* called her Jennifer. As if he were different from everyone else, wouldn't call her the same name everyone else used. Sometimes, she wondered if it meant that she was someone special to him. More than once he'd looked at her as if he wanted her—but he wanted so many women, and she wasn't about to become one of his ladies.

It was a good thing he called her Jennifer. It reminded her of Lance, kept her on guard.

She made herself remember Lance as she checked her face in the mirror above the sink, making sure there was no sign of tears. She'd been seventeen, so much in love, so desperately in love with him. She'd given him everything, held nothing back when he asked. She'd been happy, ecstatic, touching the clouds in her new love, in the sudden awareness of her own womanhood, the knowledge that she would never be alone again.

Her lover. He'd touched her with intimacy, told her she was the only woman he would ever want. Marriage was a word they hadn't needed to speak. Jenny had known, with foolish confidence, that Lance was hers for ever.

For ever. Until the night she told him that she was expecting a child...their child.

Then had come the loneliness, the emptiness. Aunt Georgina had found her crying once. After that, Jenny had kept the tears inside, grown a wall around the hurt until she could hardly feel it.

She wouldn't cry now, either. This was nothing, only a fantasy she sometimes gave way to, thinking of Jake touching her with love. He'd never know about it; no one would.

Jenny walked silently back into the entrance hallway. Silence from the living-room. She held the hanger with one hand as she slipped her coat off it, careful not to let the metal hanger make a noise as it swung free of the coat.

'Where are you going?'

Jake, moving towards the door, prowling, like a tiger. Keeping tabs on her again.

'Why?' she demanded, thrusting her chin out aggressively.

He laughed, but she knew he was irritated. 'Just answer, Jennifer. Don't evade. Don't turn my question back on me. Where are you going?'

'Out.' She didn't care how angry she made him. She wanted him to be angry. She caught herself breathing quick and shallow again, preparing for angry words she'd never intended to say.

His eyes narrowed, watching her. He spoke quickly, 'I'm sorry, Jennifer, but there's nobody else who can get that film ready for shooting. As soon as we get it done, you can have your time—take an extra week if you like.'

'I'm not angry.' He knew she was lying, but she didn't care. 'Jake, step aside, please. I'm going out.'

His face hardened. He planted himself more firmly in her path, the muscles of his thighs tensed against his trousers. She felt tension all through him. 'It's late. You can't go prowling around Vancouver alone at this time of night.'

She laughed bitterly. 'Can't I? I'm a big girl, Jake.'

'Coffee's ready!' Monica's soft call came from the living-room, where she was setting out a tray with cups and coffee.

He grasped her arm roughly, holding her back. 'Jennifer——'

She jerked away. 'What makes you think I'm going to be alone?'

Why was he so angry, so aggressively determined to keep her in the apartment?

Monica came up and linked her arm with Jake's, smiling a query.

Jenny said, 'I'm just going out for a bit. See you later.' Then she left quickly, while Monica was still clinging to his arm.

She couldn't seem to get warm, even when the car heater started blasting at her. She drove to the studio and found it cold there, too.

It was Friday night. No time to be working, but she knew she couldn't do anything else tonight. Where else could she go to be alone? She turned on the computer, dialled up Datapac and tried to pretend she wanted to be sitting at a cold computer console doing research.

When a key turned in the door, she didn't pause. She was ready for him now. She was calm again, able to tell herself that it didn't matter who Jake married or didn't marry.

She didn't look up, because she wasn't quite *that* calm.

'I thought you were out with your George?' He was leaning against the doorway, watching her thoughtfully. 'Or Wayne?'

She bent her head, her long hair dropping like a curtain between them. She touched a key to get a printout of the data on the screen. The noise of the printer covered her failure to answer him.

'You should be home in bed, Jennifer.'

'So should you.'

She still wouldn't look at him, but she could hear the smile in his voice. 'I guess we're both crazy,' he said, touching her shoulder briefly with his hand as he walked past her. Then he was sitting at the easel on the far side of the room, sketching something as if he would lose it if he didn't get it on paper quickly.

They worked together without talking for over an hour. When Jenny made a pot of tea, Jake didn't seem to notice the steaming mug that appeared beside him, although he absently picked it up later.

He was working, drawing dark black lines on the design he had sketched. She stood beside him for a moment after she put the tea down. She could smell his aftershave faintly—he was using a different scent tonight. Perhaps something Monica had given him.

She had an urge to touch him, to make him look at her.

If she did, he'd have a question in his eyes. Yes? What did you want, Jennifer?

She had no answer, so she went back to the computer console, dialled up Datapac again and started asking for more information. Jake's Datapac bill would be colossal this month.

A few minutes later, she looked over and saw him slipping out of his suit jacket, tossing it towards a nearby chair without looking to see if it had landed.

He held his shoulders stiffly. She could see the muscles moving through his light shirt. If she were Monica, she'd walk over and massage his shoulders, soothe the stiffness away.

What was wrong with her these last couple of days? All these years, she'd kept her crazy attraction to him under control. Now, suddenly, she kept looking, imagining, wanting. She couldn't seem to stop herself.

He didn't notice when she picked up his jacket, hanging it on the coat-rack near the door. He didn't look up until she put on her own coat.

'Going home?' He dropped the pen, leaning back as if he were giving up for the night, too.

'Yes.' She slid her hands into the pockets, feeling for her keys. 'I'll be back in tomorrow.'

'I won't.' He kneaded the back of his neck with one hand, wincing as he did. 'I'm going over to Victoria for the weekend.'

She said tonelessly, 'I know, Monica told me.'

'Do you want me to drive you home?' He stood up, started looking around.

'Your jacket's here on the hook,' she told him. He spotted it then and nodded, moving towards her and the jacket. Self-consciously, she stepped back. 'I don't need a ride. I've got my car. Don't stop working.'

'It's all right.' He looked back at the easel, nodding to himself. 'I've got it now. I had an idea—I had to get it on paper.' She shook off a fanciful idea that he was lonely, that he didn't want her to go yet.

He took his jacket off the hook, his eyes watching her with a terrible intensity. 'Jennifer, you've been acting oddly these last couple of days. Is everything all right with you?'

Surely there was no way that he could know how she really felt? She said firmly, 'I'm fine. It was a bit of a surprise seeing George again.' The distraction worked. He frowned at George's name and she buttoned her coat right up to the neck, shivering again. 'Jake?'

'What?' he asked absently.

She hesitated, but she had to know. 'Are you going to marry Monica?'

Jake's eyes were too darkly shuttered. Jenny hadn't a chance of seeing his expression. She felt his sudden stillness, knew he was watching her with a look she couldn't interpret. She looked down at the buttons of her coat, absently undoing the top one, then doing it back up again.

'Am I going to marry Monica?' he repeated slowly, thoughtfully. 'Yes, I probably will.'

She didn't answer. She had thought she was prepared, but she hadn't really believed it was true. She felt her face grow stiff, knew that she mustn't let him see. She bent over her buttons again, then turned her collar up and moved towards the door.

'Jennifer——' She heard him move behind her. She grasped the door-handle and turned it. She had to get away from him, quickly.

'Goodnight, Jake.'

CHAPTER THREE

JAKE slammed the door and erupted into the office, his camera and attaché case tangling with the overcoat slung over his arm. In the next room, Jenny stopped pretending to concentrate on the notes in front of her. She'd been waiting all morning for Jake to come in.

Last night she'd tried to convince herself that she didn't care who Jake married. In spite of Hans, in spite of her own relegation to the drudgery jobs this last year, she didn't want to stop working for Jake!

Some time in the night, before the sun rose again, she'd finally admitted to herself that she couldn't bear to watch Jake and Monica making their life together. She didn't know exactly when it had happened, but she'd fallen in love with Jake.

Now she had to get herself far away from him. Thank God for George!

'Jennifer? Where are you?'

She clenched her hands together, and called out, 'I'm in here! In the library.' He came around the corner, wet with rain and smiling, half laughing over something he was about to tell her. 'Jake, I've got to talk to you about——'

'I've got some great footage on that City Hall demonstration—just have a look at this videotape!'

Startled, she asked, 'What demonstration?'

'A delegation turned up at City Hall, leading a cow into the council chambers—protesting against re-zoning to put a slaughterhouse in their neighbourhood. The whole thing descended into chaos! Police, aldermen, the Mayor! One of the demonstrators threw a pitcher of water at Gerstch, and Gerstch is suing for assault. Can you believe it? Gerstch's supporters are picketing City Hall.'

'And the cow?'

He grinned widely, revealing a deep dimple in his chin. 'I think the cows have been arrested—they left, led away by two city police officers. It's going to hit the national news tonight. I've already got it sold to both networks. Oh, and that crazy woman, who wants to pass a law about couples kissing in Stanley Park, is trying to propose a motion to ban cows in City Hall.'

'It sounds like a circus.'

'Edit this tape, will you?' He dropped the tape on to her desk. She could see the excitement still gleaming in his dark eyes. 'I need a short—about five minutes—for the networks. The sensational stuff, commentary——' He spread his hands out in an all-encompassing gesture of the work he wanted her to do. 'You know the routine. Then deliver it for me, please, Jennifer. I'm going over to the North Shore—— Yes, Charlotte? What is it?'

Charlotte was hovering, holding out a pink slip of paper to Jake. 'Your lawyer called—he called twice. He needs your signature on a contract.'

He said briskly, 'You call him. Tell him I'll drop by tomorrow morning.'

'And Monica called,' Charlotte added, revealing a second pink slip.

'I'll call her back later. Remind me when I get back from the North Shore. No!' He waved her away. 'Don't tell me the rest of the messages! Anything that can't keep 'til tomorrow?'

Charlotte frowned at the papers in her hands. 'Well, no, but——'

'Then leave them for tomorrow. Too busy today. Jennifer, you look after anything that won't hold. I——'

'Jake——' If she meant to go through with it, she would have to make him listen now. Jenny insisted, 'Jake, I've got to talk to you. *Now!*'

He shook his head, turning away as he said, 'Not now. Tomorrow morning. I'm off now.'

She followed him out through the outer office. *'Jake, it can't wait!'*

'Impossible. If tomorrow won't do, call me at home tonight. Charlotte, send some flowers to Monica for me—and a note.' He stopped suddenly. Jenny was following him so closely that she almost crashed into him. He looked down at her with a sudden, penetrating intensity. 'How's George?'

'George is fine.' she answered impatiently. 'Charlotte's waiting to know what to put in Monica's note.'

He blinked. 'Oh, yes. Ah——' He looked at Charlotte, said, 'Sorry, darling. Can't get away tonight. Thanks for a lovely weekend. Love, Jake. How's that?' he asked Jenny with a smile.

Charlotte turned away. So did Jake. If she didn't stop him now, it could be days before she got another chance. Desperate to stop him, she found herself shouting, *'Jake! I'm quitting!'*

There was a sudden, total silence as Jenny's words echoed. Charlotte's jaw dropped, showing her gold-capped tooth. Jake didn't say a word, just grabbed her arm and dragged her across the office in three short steps, then pushed her into the studio and slammed the door behind them, closing Charlotte out—and Jenny in, alone with Jake.

'All right,' he said grimly. 'You've got my attention now. Let's have it.'

She took a deep breath. With his eyes boring into her, it was harder to sound firm. She'd *never* seen him look quite so threatening, his cheekbones jutting out sharply under glowering eyes. She remembered suddenly that his

Haida ancestors had been warriors feared everywhere on the Pacific coast.

'Let go of me, Jake! You're hurting my arm. You heard what I said.' She sucked in a deep breath. 'I'm quitting. I quit.'

'You can't quit,' he said flatly. 'I won't let you.'

'You can't stop me,' insisted Jenny, with a conviction she couldn't quite feel.

He loosened his grip on her arm, but she knew it would tighten again if she made a move. Impatiently, he said, 'Let's get to the point, shall we? What's your grievance?'

'Grievance?' She shook her head, confusion showing in her eyes for a moment, then anger. 'I'm just trying to tell you that I'm quitting—I've been *trying* to tell you all morning, but you won't stay still long enough for me to get out a word!'

He grimaced. 'You didn't have any trouble out there just now. You got your message through. I take it this is about your holidays. I honestly don't know how we can——'

She stamped her foot in frustration. '*It isn't the bloody holidays!* Oh, partly I suppose it is—and a lot of other things, too. But it doesn't make any difference now. I'm leaving. I'll get the organising done for the Eglinton thing—then *I'm leaving.*'

She'd never seen him so much at a loss before. He'd fallen silent, staring at her as if he didn't know how to handle this. She pushed down a strong urge to change her mind, tell him it was all a mistake.

In the next room, Charlotte was phoning the florists with Jake's love message for Monica. Staying wouldn't change that.

She made her voice businesslike. 'You were going to the North Shore?'

'*To hell with the North Shore!*' he exploded. 'What's this *really* about? Someone else offered you a job? How much, Jennifer? How much were you offered? If it's a raise you're after——'

'It's *not* money. It's not another job.'

'Then *what is it*, for God's sake?' He turned angrily away from her, then spun back, coming too close. She could feel the violence and frustration radiating off his body in waves.

'Jake, stop shouting at me!'

He took a deep breath. Jenny's hands clenched. She'd never seen him so angry before. His blazing eyes made a lie of the flat calmness in his voice. 'Why are you leaving?'

Lamely, she said, 'I'm going away,' then added, 'Sailing. With George.'

'George again?' He glared at her for long seconds, then said, 'All right. Have your fling—your damned holidays! But cut this nonsense about leaving! *You can't leave!*'

He moved closer. She stepped back, moving around her desk and almost falling into her chair. She felt sick, weak from the strain of shouting at Jake and having him shout at her.

'I'm really going,' she insisted, not looking at him. 'I'm *not* coming back.'

'Just like that?' He waved an arm, gesturing at her desk, the worktable they often used together. His motion caught her attention and she found herself looking into his eyes, seeing an unexpected vulnerability that was quickly shuttered as he said, 'Five years—and you're just going to leave?'

Tonelessly, she explained, 'I've got a month's holiday starting next week. You promised me that last winter. In January, you said——'

'I remember what I said, for God's sake!'

'Don't swear at me!' she shouted back.

He didn't lower his voice either as he retorted, 'You're in a temper today, aren't you, my lady? What's got into you?'

'Look who's talking!' She met his blazing eyes head on. 'You're prowling around like an angry bear—roaring like one, too!'

He paced across the room and back again, demanding, 'Are you marrying this George?' He lunged around her desk, grabbing her shoulders and giving a short, rough shake. *'Jennifer, are you?'*

'Damn it, Jake! Let *go* of me! You're hurting! And it's none of your business!' She jerked back from his hands, sending her chair rolling away from him. She eyed him warily, nervous of his violent anger.

'Are you marrying George?'

She couldn't help a nervous giggle. 'I don't think George is going to ask me.' Then her smile died as his face darkened in fury. For a minute she thought he was going to explode, then he stepped back and his face relaxed into a shuttered mask.

'I don't believe it,' he said flatly. 'If someone had got through that damned reserve of yours, I'd know it.' He frowned, studying her, asking, 'So what is it? It's not like you to let your love-life interfere with your career. There's got to be more to it.'

She shifted papers on her desk, managed to sound indifferent, almost bored. 'If it amuses you to speculate, then go ahead.'

'Jennifer, you can't just take off into the unknown with some man—this isn't your style, a cheap affair!'

'A cheap——' She pushed the chair back again and stood up, facing him, glaring at those eyes as the angry brown fires overtook the coolness she'd seen a moment ago. 'Look here, Jake, you're not my keeper! And you're the last one to talk about cheap affairs!'

'Well, *someone* sure as hell should be your keeper! You're throwing away your career—*everything*—for a shoddy romance. Do your parents have any idea what you're doing?'

Her parents! God! She closed her eyes to cover the moment's hurt at his assumption that her parents would care. 'I'm not exactly a child. I'm twenty-eight years old.'

'You're sure as hell not behaving like it!'

'Thanks a lot!' she shouted angrily. 'You're not interested in my well-being! You're thinking of yourself. It'll put your schedule out of whack if I quit.'

'That's the understatement of the year! It'd be chaos and you know it. How the——'

'Will you stop swearing?'

He glared at her, then took a deep breath. 'All right. How would you suggest I go about replacing you? *Damn* it, Jennifer! You're necessary here!'

'What you really mean,' she said slowly and bitterly, 'is that no one else around here wants to give up all their holidays, their weekends and evenings, just to make sure you keep the commitments you take on. You say I'm giving up my career! Well, just what am I giving up?' She jabbed a finger hard on to the desk. 'A lifetime as your general dogsbody? I don't go on location any more. I don't get to film anything except greasy hamburgers— Jake, a couple of years ago you wouldn't have taken on junk like that! You're doing more and more, without thinking about the quality of what you're doing, giving me all the dirty work, and yourself and Hans the assignments that have some excitement. You're getting bigger, but you're *not* getting better!'

Silence fell around them as her words echoed in the studio. Jake stared at her, his brown face strangely pale.

'If that's how you felt, you should have said so long ago, shouldn't you? Instead of hiding your thoughts behind those green eyes.'

'Jake, I don't——'

But he was going, turning away, closing that damned door quietly for once, but with a decisive click that made it impossible for her to go after him.

He didn't even know the colour of her eyes, saying they were green. They were hazel, plain old hazel.

She'd always known it would be a mistake to start shouting at Jake, that she would say too much. It was a good thing he'd left when he did, before she'd said even more.

She felt sick now. She'd seen Jake angry often enough, although usually at other people. He'd never hesitated to speak his mind to anyone; but no matter what Jake had said, she'd kept any angry retorts deeply hidden.

She met George for lunch.

'I'm going nuts!' George confessed over a plate of salad. 'I've got a shopping list for the boat a mile long, and I can't find half the stuff I need. Lanterns, for example—you'd think in a city this size I could find brass lanterns for a boat! Are you all right? How did the chieftain take your news?'

'Badly. My ears are still burning!' She shrugged, smiled unconvincingly and asked, 'Shouldn't you be calling your boat a yacht?'

'Too classy for me,' said her elegant cousin. 'I'm a down-to-earth lady.' She shovelled a hefty forkful of salad into her dainty mouth. 'Somehow, I thought you'd change your mind at the last minute. Tell me the details. How did the big scene go?'

'As you say, it was a big scene ... At first he thought I was blackmailing him for my holidays, then he accused me of taking a job with the competition. He offered me more money.'

'Much more?' asked George curiously. 'If he wanted you badly enough——'

'We didn't get into dollars and cents.' Jake's angry, frustrated face was burned into her mind. 'I said I was going sailing with you. He asked if I was going to marry you.'

George choked on her lettuce.

Jenny said defensively, 'Well, I just said George.'

'Your cousin George?'

'No.' She shook her head, smiling slightly. 'Just George.'

'Oh!' George smiled, a piece of lettuce dangling just inches from her mouth. 'Now, why did you let him think that?'

'What difference does it make who he thinks I'm with?'

'He was jealous,' George decided with satisfaction.

'Of course he wasn't jealous!' Jenny flushed, remembering the feel of Jake's eyes on her, the times when she'd looked up and seen his awareness of her as a woman. To George, she muttered, 'He goes through women the way you go through shoes. I suppose there have been times when I could have been one of them.' That look in his eyes, almost as if he were daring her to let him get closer.

'You're in love with him, aren't you?'

'*No!*' she denied too swiftly.

'Is that why you're coming with me, Jenny? If you're in love with him, you shouldn't run away.'

'It's not that—it's everything, everyone around me. I feel as if my whole life is shrinking, as if I'm watching everyone else's life. Wayne going to Saudi Arabia. Mom and Dad in the Caribbean. Chris Eglinton climbing his mountains.' And Jake and Monica.

George shook her head, confused. 'Chris—who?'

'A documentary we're doing,' Jenny explained. 'He's nobody, really, just another person doing his thing.'

'So it's Jenny's turn?'

'Yes.' She had to remember that. Jake was going to make this difficult for her, but she would just have to hold on to her determination to do her own thing for once. Jenny's turn.

She was in love with him, but surely it would fade, go away. She didn't want to love him. Loving only brought pain ...

'I'll see you next week,' she had said to Lance as he dropped her at her aunt's house that last night.

He'd nodded, saying nothing. She'd felt a sudden fear. She'd flown into his arms, clinging, her intense young voice declaring, 'I love you so much!' as if she were afraid he didn't know.'

She'd never seen him again.

She looked up from her memories, and saw George watching her too intently.

They had already arranged their schedule. Jenny would fly north the following Sunday, with George meeting her at the airport in a rental car.

She wouldn't see George again for a week. It was going to be a busy week, trying to get everything done for Jake before she left him. If she was busy enough, she might be able to avoid another confrontation scene with him.

She stayed away all afternoon, working in the library, making phone calls from a pay phone instead of going back to the office. It was late by the time she went back to the studio.

She looked for his car outside the office building, but didn't see it. Still on the North Shore, or perhaps his lawyer had caught up with him for the signatures he needed. Since Jake had won the award for his film on the Swiftsure Race, he'd been busier and busier, so flooded with commercial contracts that he could hardly stop and work on the exciting, creative projects that had been typical of the first four years Jenny worked with him.

It had all happened together: The award, the flood of new commercial contracts, Hans being hired as Jake's assistant. *Jenny's discontent.*

And Jake's. He'd always been volatile, but Jenny was sure the commercial success of the last year had been bad for him. His time was increasingly taken up with petty details like scheduling and politics. There was less and less opportunity for him to do truly creative work.

Yet he couldn't seem to turn down a new contract, no matter how mundane. He accepted them, then handed the worst jobs to Jenny. He'd go nuts, thought Jenny, finishing the Madison series on his own.

Hamburgers!

She really *had* to get away, get some perspective, prove to herself that there was more to life than holding Jake's spare film cassettes. *Or watching Jake and Monica.*

She'd never believed he'd really marry any of the women he dated. Had he *really* shared his inner self with Monica? Jake the artist, the passionately caring man; whenever she'd seen him with a woman, he'd seemed to hold some part of himself aside.

Yet he'd let Jenny see the private part of him. Crazy, but she thought she knew things about him that no one else did. In some ways, she'd been closer to him than any of his women.

Did Monica know that he'd cried the night his grandfather had died? Jenny had been with him that night, sitting in the studio in the dark, listening to Jake share his memories of the old chief who had just died. Jenny had cried, too.

It really was time she left, got away from him. She was becoming obsessed with Jake. She came into the studio feeling his presence, knowing he would be sitting at his desk. Heaven knew where his car was, but Jake was right here.

He was staring at a mound of paperwork that had been growing over the last few weeks. His gaze shifted to her as she came in, but his face remained blank, as if he didn't really see her.

'Where were you?' he asked tonelessly.

'The library.'

'I thought you'd gone.'

His eyes flickered to the coat-rack where her umbrella still hung, down to her spare pair of shoes on the shoe-rack. Whatever he said, he'd known she'd be back.

She carried her armful of books and papers over to her desk, her back tense, aware of his eyes on her.

Her ears must be supersensitive. She heard the thin lead of his pencil snap.

Tension crept into his voice as he asked, 'Exactly when are you planning to leave me?'

She arranged the papers carefully, answered, 'My plane leaves on Sunday afternoon.'

'Your plane?'

He clicked another lead down on his pencil. She sat down, finally looking across at him. His black hair covered his forehead; he was looking down, sketching something, perhaps, though she thought he was just doodling. Another time she might have walked over to look. She slid open a drawer and placed her pens carefully in the slot where they belonged.

'George's boat is in Alaska. I'm flying to Alaska on Sunday.'

His pencil snapped again. He crumpled the paper and threw it into the waste-paper basket beside his desk.

'Will you have the preparations ready for the Eglinton film by then? And the Madison series?'

'I think I'll have Eglinton ready.' She kept her voice neutral. 'You have to make some decisions about sched-uling before I can go farther, but if we could hash those out tomorrow I think I can get all the reservations set up, supplies lists, and so forth. I can't get Madison done—I'll finish the film I was working on, but the last two will have to be done by someone else.'

She waited for a storm of protest from him, but he said nothing, just turned back to his paperwork and proceeded to ignore her.

So she went home and spent the evening dreading coming back to work the next morning, facing a surly, disapproving Jake for the rest of the week.

But the next morning Jake was gone long before she arrived. He'd left only a note.

> Back Friday. Schedule Eglinton shooting however you want.
>
> Jake

Jenny spent her last week in relative isolation. Monica had gone to Toronto on a week-long conference on child care, and wouldn't be back until after Jenny had left. George had flown back to Alaska to provision the yacht. Jake was—— Heaven knew where Jake was, but she was glad she didn't have to face him every day.

She thought about calling her parents, but felt too depressed to face a conversation with her mother.

She tried to get her mind into gear, planning freelance articles and videos she might do after she left Jake, but even that seemed meaningless.

Jake returned on Friday afternoon, almost quietly, murmuring something to Charlotte, saying a few low words to Hans that sent him hurrying out with a camera.

Jenny was printing carefully and neatly on to a videotape label. When Jake came into the room, he closed the door behind him quietly. Her hand jerked and she watched a messy squiggle appear in the middle of the label. This was getting to be a habit of hers, messing up labels as Jake came in.

She peeled off a new label and fixed it carefully over the ruined one with shaking hands, then put the tape down, knowing she couldn't write again while he was watching her.

He stood just inside the door, leaning back against it. His face was always deeply lined, as if the intensity with which he lived had drawn itself upon his features. Today the lines seemed even deeper. His dark face had a grey tinge, as she'd seen once or twice before when he was catching 'flu or a bad cold.

'Jake, you've been going without sleep.'

He shrugged her concern away, and said tonelessly, 'I was tied up last night with that environmental group in Williams Lake, then I had to catch an early flight.'

He was examining her desk with a long, slow look that didn't miss anything. The shiny, just-cleaned surface. The empty in-basket. The drawers were empty, too, although that didn't show.

'So you're all ready to go?'

'Yes.' He looked so terribly tired. She wished she could tell him to go home and go to bed.

'Eglinton?' he asked, his voice hardening.

'It's ready. On your desk.'

He walked over, not sitting, but standing behind his chair, turning the pages while he stood looking down, reading, then meeting her eyes across the room. Nervously, she picked up the tape again.

'Put that down. You're just fiddling with it.'

She dropped the tape with a clatter. 'You're staring at me. You're making me nervous.'

He said, bitterly, 'I always make you nervous, don't I, Jennifer?'

'*No*, you—I just don't know what you're planning to do. You come in here and shut the door, and you look——'

'What?'

'*I don't know!*' she wailed. 'Angry?'

'I suppose that's right. I am angry.' He stood up swiftly, starting to prowl now. 'Are you all packed?'

'Pretty well.'

'Monica said you're giving up your share of the apartment?'

'Yes.'

'Do you need help moving anything?' He wasn't looking at her, but she sensed anger behind his quiet questions.

'No.' Did they have to have this meaningless, painful exchange of words? Some of her distress came through in her voice as she explained, 'Monica's storing some boxes for me in the storeroom. All that's left to take are a couple of suitcases.'

He pushed his hands into his pockets, stared out of the window at something. 'What does Monica think of your going off with this George fellow?'

'I didn't ask her.' Jenny hadn't told Monica anything about George. What a crazy fiction she had created in letting Jake think George was a man! 'Ask her yourself.'

He frowned at her. 'What about your car? Are you selling it?'

'No. Monica's going to use it.'

'So you might come back to Vancouver? Aren't you sure of George? Is he going to discard you when you've——'

She closed her eyes briefly on a sudden wave of painful memories. 'Jake, let's not get into an argument again. I don't——'

He said abruptly, 'I'll give you a ride to the airport.'

'I'm taking a taxi,' she decided in a rush.

'Don't be silly!' He swung back from the window, his hands pushed deeper into his pockets. 'We're friends, aren't we? I always thought we were.'

'Yes,' she whispered. God, she was going to miss him!

'So I'll see you off on your plane,' he said decisively, his tone allowing no argument. 'What time shall I pick you up?'

She closed her eyes briefly again, realising that she couldn't avoid this. He was going to come for her, drive her to the airport. And he hadn't given up yet. She could sense a dangerous determination in him.

Thank goodness for George! If Jake insisted on trying to persuade her to stay, maybe Jenny could pull off a convincing act of a girl determined to throw everything over for love.

CHAPTER FOUR

'JAKE, what are you doing? I thought we were going out for dinner?' Monica's voice was still soft, but somehow a thin edge of frustration was finding its way through.

'In a minute.' Jake pointed the remote control at his television and punched the channel button grimly, switching through several channels. A stream of pictures flashed past—a car flying over a cliff and bursting into flames, a baby-faced blonde holding a bottle of shampoo and simpering at someone off-camera. The picture settled on a depressed young man who talked with forced enthusiasm.

Monica protested, 'That's a sports broadcast. You're not a football enthusiast.'

'Depends who's playing.' Jake frowned heavily at the sports announcer. 'The weather's next.'

Storms in the Gulf of Alaska. He'd caught just the tail end of a marine weather update when he'd turned on the radio in his car half an hour ago. Monica had been settling her skirts into the bucket seat of Jake's sports car, still talking about the play they had just seen. Jake had heard the words 'gale warning' as the volume came up on the car speaker, but Monica's voice had drowned the rest.

Where was Jenny now? Did that lover of hers have any idea how to handle a boat in a storm? He shouldn't have let her go. He should have done more, somehow made her see that sailing around the north Pacific in a small sailboat wasn't a game.

'Are we going out?' Monica asked patiently.

'In a few minutes,' he answered absently. 'I want to catch the weather.'

Monica waved a hand towards his living-room window. 'You can *see* the weather. Rain! You dashed back here as if you had a devil on your tail. Driving like a maniac, breaking the speed limit, then——'

'I heard there was a storm in the Gulf of Alaska.' He was sitting on the edge of a large chair, glaring at the announcer.

'It's Jenny? You're worried about Jenny?'

He used the controls to turn the volume up, then back down. His face was grim as he said, 'That's my part of the country. I grew up on the Queen Charlotte Islands—summers, anyway. My mother's family were mostly fishermen. I spent my summers fishing, finding out just how wild those waters can be.'

'Jenny can look after herself.'

Jake turned away angrily, remembering Jennifer sitting in that coffee shop at the airport the day she left. She'd agreed to let him drive her to the airport and they had come out from the city in silence, Jenny staring out of the window, presumably dreaming of her damned George. Jake had pretended to concentrate on the traffic while he tried to think of a way to talk sense into her.

He couldn't believe she would throw up everything for a man whose name he'd never even heard until a few days ago.

In the five years since she'd walked into his studio, he'd seen her work her way through a string of admirers. He'd watched jealously, yet never believed any of them mattered to her. She kept them all at a distance. Certainly he had never thought Jennifer might leave him for one of them. She was too damned *good* at her job to just walk away like that.

But she had done it, and only unwillingly accepted his offer of a ride to the airport. She'd insisted on dragging one of the heavy suitcases into the terminal building on her own, until he'd grabbed it away from her and stalked to the ticket counter. He had slid both suitcases on to the scales with a muscular ease that he would never have admitted was a deliberate show of superior strength.

She'd had a routine conversation with the woman at the counter—Yes, two pieces of luggage. Non-smoking—no, not a window seat.

In the course of work, Jennifer had often flown with him to locations where he was filming. She had always arranged to let Jake have the window seat, placing herself in an aisle seat. If he thought of it at all, he had assumed she gave him the window seat because she knew he enjoyed looking out as they flew. Now, after five years, it occurred to him that she was nervous of flying, that she had always been oddly silent when they were in the air.

How on earth could she be afraid to fly, yet willing to trust a man named George to pilot her over the high seas?

'Gate twenty-nine, four o'clock,' the ticket clerk pronounced.

Jenny took her boarding pass and slipped it into her shoulder-bag, swinging back to Jake, eager to take her leave and get on her way to that blasted George.

She was dressed casually for travelling—jeans and a light blouse under a loose sweater that hinted enticingly at the fullness of her breasts. He kept finding his eyes straying to the tightness of the denim across her hips, the curves revealed by the soft sweater.

'Thanks for the ride, Jake.' She stepped out of the way of a young woman lugging a toddler and two suitcases.

Jake stared down at her, wishing he could take her in his arms, realising that she really *was* going. He had no idea how he could make her see reason. He'd never been able to get close to her except when they were working.

'Thanks,' Jennifer said again. He wondered why she was so nervous of him. 'I'll go to the gate now. I may as well.'

'You've got an hour. Let's go have a coffee.' He grasped her elbow and steered her out of the path of a volubly French group wheeling past with two luggage carts piled high with suitcases. He avoided her eyes, knowing she wasn't coming willingly. 'Are you hungry, Jennifer? Did you have lunch?'

She shook her head and he urged her on, propelling her ahead of him.

'Here, let's get out of this crowd. All of Vancouver must be flying today. Now, which? You're not hungry? Or you didn't have lunch?'

'It doesn't matter. They'll feed me on the plane.'

Once he had her seated in the restaurant, he ordered her a light lunch and she didn't protest. She sat staring silently out of the window. He had to work at distracting her.

'Did you see the photographers gathering near the CP International ticket counter?'

She had shaken her head, making him uncomfortably aware that she didn't want to be with him.

'I wonder who they're waiting for,' he persisted. 'Someone said something about the Prime Minister's wife.'

'I doubt that. She probably travels on government jets all the time.'

'Don't be cynical, Jennifer,' he had teased and, finally, she had laughed.

'Jennifer, do you—what are your plans for this sailing trip? Your itinerary? This George, does he know what he's doing? Now, don't get prickly, Jenn—lord, you're temperamental these days. I'm just concerned about you.'

He hadn't often heard impatience in her voice, but now she said abruptly, 'I've sailed before, Jake. I grew up sailing, spending my summers on the water.'

'At Campbell River, for God's sake!' he burst out angrily, frustrated by his inability to make her see reason.

She bristled, pushed her hair back and said aggressively, 'I'll have you know that we've had some pretty heavy weather up there.'

'That's protected waters,' he scoffed. 'Sure, the winds blow, but you never get the kind of seas they get in the Dixon Entrance—where are you going, Jennifer? The boat's in Ketchikan?' She nodded and he pressed on, 'What's your first port of call after you leave? When are you leaving?'

She looked across the table, away from him. He followed her gaze. She was looking out of the window at the runway. Was she in that much of a hurry to get to her lover? She said, 'Jake, our plans aren't that definite. We're probably stopping at the Queen Charlotte Islands—it's the logical first stop, just across the Dixon Entrance.'

His overactive imagination supplied a graphic vision of the two of them, drifting in some secluded bay, in intimate loneliness. Monica, he reminded himself grimly, trying to drown out one fantasy with another. It didn't work. It never did. He was cursed with wanting the one woman who wouldn't let him near.

'*Just!* Jennifer, do you have any idea what that stretch of water can be like?'

'Jake, I——'

He leaned forward, pleaded, 'Shouldn't you think about this more? After all, this George is a pretty new event in your life. You're throwing over everything for someone you hardly know.'

She stared at him for a long, heavy minute. When she did answer, her voice was flat and angry.

'You're making a lot of assumptions, aren't you, Jake? I haven't told you anything, but you're determined to jump to conclusions. First, you've got me taking a job with your competition, then running off on a sudden— a sudden love affair. None of it's your business, but— just as a point of information, I've known George a lot longer than I've known you.'

'I don't believe it,' he insisted over a sick fear. Why the hell did it matter to him? She'd never been even slightly interested in him as a man. He wanted her back because he needed her in the studio. This sexual attraction would go away sooner or later. He found himself insisting, 'I don't believe in this love affair with George.'

She'd always been so cool. He'd seen the ice in her eyes when she caught him watching her, when she'd sensed his attraction to her. He'd seen her with other men, and he would have sworn it was the same. She kept everyone at a distance.

Was George the reason for it all? For George, was she a passionate lover, giving out the warmth, the passion he sometimes thought he sensed in her?

'You don't believe——' Jennifer started to say angrily, then her voice lost its heat, dropped. 'But it doesn't matter what you believe, does it?' She smiled without any humour. 'Excuse me for a minute.'

He should have realised what she was up to, but he actually thought she was going to the ladies' room. He watched her, then jerked to his feet as she went through the doors to the main terminal and just kept walking.

She'd left him tied up with a furious waitress who was just bringing a seafood salad and clam chowder to their table. The waitress was quickly reinforced by the restaurant manager, an aggressively dangerous woman dressed in a severe grey suit. Jake managed to free himself from the whole embarrassing incident with quick apologies and ready cash.

Jennifer was nowhere in sight.

'Damn!' he cursed under his breath, earning himself a severe reprimand from an elderly woman who rushed past with her handbag clutched tightly to her breast.

What had got into Jennifer, transforming her from her usual quiet, helpful, dependable stability into—into what? He'd always known she was hiding her feelings from him, but he hadn't expected this strangely contrary woman who seemed to be determined to do the craziest, the most——

He caught up with her just as she was passing through the security checkpoint.

'Jennifer!'

She ignored him, smiling brightly at the guard as she handed him her handbag.

Jake moved between Jennifer and the security booth. 'Now, listen——'

'Your boarding pass, sir?'

The uniformed man stepped between them as Jennifer walked briskly through the X-ray scan.

'I'm not a passenger. I just want to talk to——'

'Sorry, sir. You can't go beyond this point without a boarding pass.'

And Jennifer was gone, walking around the corner, with only a quick, unrepentant glance back.

Now, two weeks later, Jake stared at the television set, not hearing the details of today's football game, but waiting for what he'd come for. The weather. Just how detailed did they get on this channel? He couldn't re-member, hadn't ever really cared before.

'Are we going out?' Monica asked, not for the first time.

'Yes,' he said absently, wishing he'd never started dating her. 'In a few minutes.'

What a fool he'd made of himself in that flaming airport! Jennifer, turning contrary and elusive, had been like a red flag to a bull. First the embarrassment in the restaurant, then leaving him standing like a fool at that security check.

Damn! No one had made a fool of him since the day he'd gone to art school over the protests of his father's family. Only Jennifer, damn her! He'd never been able to get anywhere near her. Was that why she'd held such a fascination for him from the beginning?

When Jennifer first started working for him, he'd been in the middle of a casual affair. He'd ended it immediately, turning his attention to this mysteriously quiet girl with the deep, stubborn eyes.

She'd said no when he'd asked her to dinner—but she'd accepted an invitation from the accountant in the office downstairs. When she stopped dating the accountant, Jake had tried again, inviting her to a show he knew she wanted to see.

She had been silent for a long moment, concentrating on the papers in front of her. Then she had met his eyes directly and said, 'I don't think it's a good idea.'

He hadn't asked again. He hadn't stopped wanting her, but he thought he'd stopped showing it. After a while, he came to see how valuable an assistant she was, and he told himself he was glad that he hadn't ruined a good working relationship for a short-lived affair.

But now she was leaving, walking away and leaving him on the wrong side of an airport security check. He stood staring at the empty hallway, finally becoming aware of the uniformed guard who was smiling, as if he had seen it all before.

If she thought she could walk away that easily, evade him by walking through a gate and laugh back from the other side ...

'I want a ticket on the flight to Ketchikan!' he demanded of the ticket clerk back in the terminal building. 'The one that's boarding at gate twenty-nine now.'

She touched keys, stared at her computer display. 'I have no seats on that flight, sir. If you'd like to go on standby?'

'Yes, all right. And book me back, too.'

She paused, her hand poised over the keyboard. 'On which flight, sir?'

'The same plane.'

'The same? Sir——'

'It does come back, doesn't it?'

'Yes, it comes back—immediately.' She glared at him, evidently trying to decide just how much of a nutcase he was. 'That flight only stays on the ground at Ketchikan for——'

'That's fine. Just do it, would you?' he said abruptly, embarrassed at having to explain his irrational impulse. He pushed a credit card across the counter to her, and that seemed to silence the protests. Apparently it didn't matter how crazy he was, if he was willing to pay.

Then he waited, prowling the terminal on the wrong side of the security checkpoint, watching the clock. The loudspeaker call, when it came, was difficult to hear, but he caught '…standby passengers Mudge and Austin,' and dashed back to get the boarding pass that would let him through the security checkpoint.

'No hand luggage?' asked the security guard, hiding his smile as he recognised Jake.

'No.'

'You'd better hurry, sir. Gate twenty-nine has already boarded.'

So he ran down the empty corridor, flashing his boarding pass at the stewardess, turning to ease his broad shoulders down the narrow corridor, looking for the curtain of long, brown hair that would identify Jennifer.

She was near the front, in the non-smoking section, wedged between a quietly suited businessman and a youth with a punk haircut that projected from his head in a blond-turning-purple nightmare.

'Excuse me——' he bent over the purple hair, speaking low-voiced '—I wonder if you'd mind trading seats with me, so I can sit with my wife. I'm two rows back, in 8F.'

Despite the hair, the boy smiled and nodded, pulling an oversized pack from under the seat and stumbling over Jake in his hurry to comply.

Jake had dropped into the aisle seat, his shoulders too wide for the space allotted them, pushing into Jennifer's space. He was uncomfortably aware that she shifted to move away from him. The stewardess walked back, glanced down at him with a frown, shrugged and walked on past.

'Your wife?' Jennifer's voice sounded amused. Thankfully, she wasn't looking at him; he was sure he'd flushed deeply enough that it would show even through his dark skin. He heard the anger clipping her voice. 'That's a new one. You do like to get your own way, don't you?'

She kept her eyes away from him, looking across the businessman's open copy of *Time Magazine* to the window. They were starting to move away from the terminal building. 'You do whatever it takes,' her low voice lashed him. 'Lies, flashing that charm. *Whatever it takes.*'

'I wanted to talk to you.'

She glanced at him. As usual, he couldn't read anything in her eyes as she said wryly, 'You have me as a captive audience, so have your say. You've been itching to lecture me all week. You——' She stopped talking abruptly, her hands tensed briefly as the jet accelerated. At the front of the passenger cabin, the stewardess was standing, facing the passengers as she began to demonstrate the safety features of the aeroplane. On the loudspeaker a male voice narrated an accompaniment to her motions.

He covered Jennifer's clenched hand with his. 'Why didn't you tell me you were afraid of flying?'

She jerked her hand away. 'What difference would it make? Shh! I want to hear this.'

The stewardess gave them an annoyed look. He dropped his voice. 'When we flew to California last year, you got this same demonstration and——'

'Two years ago,' she corrected. 'That was two years ago. I haven't gone anywhere with you in over a year.'

'You haven't? Surely——'

'Nowhere. Not since you hired Hans.'

'Are you sure?' He shifted uncomfortably. 'You must be. You're always right about the details—I didn't realise.'

'Didn't you?' she said coldly. 'Since the day Hans walked into your studio, I haven't gone on location anywhere.'

She was glaring at him, challenging him. He stared back, picking out the green glints in her hazel eyes. Her eyes had always concealed more than they revealed, yet sometimes he'd imagined they responded to him.

He remembered the California trip. They'd been doing a film on a Canadian expatriate who lived in California and claimed to have visions of the future.

The psychic had put them up in his large beach house. Jake had just finished a rather unsatisfactory affair with a girl named Merle, another in a string of attempts to distract himself from his futile attraction to Jennifer.

It was starting to affect his work. He supposed it was because she was so indifferent to him—some kind of arrogant male desire to be universally desired by women. He liked to think he was free of that kind of nonsense, but he was becoming obsessed by Jennifer, dreaming dreams that would have her slapping his face if she'd ever known.

He'd spent three nights sleeping in the psychic's guest bedroom, aware of Jennifer in the next room, imagining he could hear her breathing, see her sleeping. During the days, he hadn't been able to take his eyes off her, watching her move about in the thin clothes that were suitable for the hot sun, but showed every seductive curve of her body.

He hadn't slept, and he'd made a mess of the film, shooting again and again, missing the best angles, his eyes watching Jennifer when they should have been watching the viewfinder.

Despite the fact that he'd grown to depend on her so much, he'd vowed not to take her with him on the next trip.

If he saw a little less of Jennifer, perhaps he could shake this hopeless infatuation he had for her. If he could get her back in the background of his life, out of his dreams——

So he had hired Hans, ostensibly as a photographer, but actually as a buffer between himself and Jennifer.

It hadn't helped.

She was glaring at him, challenging him to deny her accusation. He couldn't tell her the truth, and he wasn't very good at lies. Weakly, he said, 'If being left behind bothered you, why didn't you say something?'

She shifted in her seat, her hair sweeping back in an angry gesture. He smelled the soft perfume from her shampoo. He wanted to touch the hair, smooth it back, see her eyes close as he covered her lips with his. Those lips moved angrily, saying, 'Jake, I *did*! I've told you that I wanted something more challenging—most recently, I asked if I couldn't get back into active film-making, and you gave me that bloody hamburger thing!'

'I didn't know you minded that much.' He'd never really thought about what she must be feeling, her reaction to Hans coming in to take over much of her job. '*Damn it, Jennifer!* Why did you have to wait until now—when you've already decided to leave—to speak your mind? You know I get busy, involved, can't concentrate on anything but the job I'm on. You, of all people, should understand that. If you had a problem, if you weren't happy about your work, you should have made me listen.'

'Now that's a good one! What was I to do? Hit you over the head with it? Stand in front of you like a road block and demand to be heard?' She was glaring at him, breathing quickly, her breasts rising and falling rapidly under the sweater.

He moved slightly closer to her and, suppressing an urge to touch his lips to her forehead, said, 'If that's what it takes, yes.'

She stared at him, hazel eyes turned black with anger. Then, suddenly, she laughed, shaking her head and saying, 'Maybe you're right, I don't know. In any case, it doesn't matter now.'

'Doesn't it? Jennifer, why are you really going on this crazy excursion? Is it George? Do you love him that much? I don't think you do. I don't think you know what you're doing. You're throwing your career away. If you're discontented with the way things are, we can work on that, change a few things.'

She stared at him intently. 'What things, Jake?'

There was something in her eyes beyond his comprehension. He shifted uncomfortably and found himself changing the subject.

'This flight wasn't booked going back when I got on. You could probably get a flight back—come back to Vancouver and spend some time thinking about this.'

'There's nothing to think about.'

Without planning to, he found himself touching her face, turning it towards him so that he could look into her eyes. 'Why are you on this plane, Jennifer? It's not like you to throw everything away so rashly. Surely——'

Her eyes dropped away, covered by long brown lashes. 'As you said the other day, you really don't know anything about me.'

'The other day, when you quit, you were screaming at me.' He couldn't get over that—Jennifer, flaming hot and screaming.

'Would you rather I screamed now?' she asked on a shaky laugh.

'It might be better.' He found himself smiling back at her, admitting, 'I'd like it. I'd know what you were thinking then. It's all a mask, isn't it, Jennifer? All that cool confidence, it's not the real Jennifer at all. What are you really thinking right now?'

Her eyes met his, sparkling half-way between laughter and anger. 'If you want the truth, I'm wishing you'd get the hell off this plane.'

He gestured to the window. 'We're thirty thousand feet high. Getting out could be a problem.'

She jerked her head abruptly, staring out of the window. 'My God, we are! I was so busy being furious with you, I didn't even notice the take-off—Jake, will you stop this crazy attempt to get me back to work? I'm not coming.'

All the arguments he had intended to use evaporated as he watched her turning away to look back out of the window.

'All right,' he said softly, wanting to bring her gaze back to him. He reached over and loosened her hand from its grip on the arm of the seat, turning it and smothering it in his own large brown hand. Hers seemed small and fragile, which struck him as odd because she had always appeared so sturdy and self-contained.

He remembered the day she had walked into his life, standing in the entrance to his studio, calmly watching while he tried to send her away. He didn't have a job for her. He was overworked and too busy to waste time on brand-new graduates who had stars in their eyes.

He'd never known exactly how it happened, but she was seated at his messy desk, straightening out his attempts to schedule what was quickly turning into a nightmare of overwork instead of a successful artistic enterprise.

Now he couldn't imagine how Austin Media could survive without her, how he could maintain his sanity and still work.

'Are you really so afraid of flying? Why didn't you tell me? We could have gone to California by train last year.'

'Two years ago,' she corrected once more, her voice businesslike, 'and that would have been silly. Yes, I'm always nervous. No, don't start telling me all the statistics about air travel being safest. I know it all, but when I'm up here I can't help feeling that I have to keep this beast in the air by effort of will … If I relax for a minute, it'll tumble to the ground.'

'Try it—just for a minute.' He could feel her hand starting to relax as he massaged the tense muscles of her fingers. He found himself wondering what else she was afraid of, wanting to slay her dragons for her.

'That's pretty risky,' she said, laughing, but still tense.

'Life is full of risks,' he said softly, taking her other hand so that they both rested in his, holding her eyes with his.

She said defensively, 'I do know how silly it is, I really do. That's why I get on these things anyway. And I won't do anything silly, like screaming or demanding to be let off. I'll just be quietly frightened.'

'Are you?' he asked.

She smiled then, shaking her head, 'Not so much now,' she admitted. 'Usually I try to get involved in a really good book the night before I fly. Then I spend the whole trip reading, pretending I'm at home in bed.'

'I'm sorry I'm not a good book,' he said then, speaking before he thought, wishing the words back when he saw her flush as she pulled her hands away from his.

He couldn't even apologise or explain, because he had meant exactly what she thought he had. He had this clear image of her, lying in his arms, the bedding tumbled around them and her eyes looking up at him with green and golden fires burning deep in their depths.

The stewardess delivered their drinks at that moment. The businessman on Jennifer's other side was apparently asleep—or pretending to be, while he listened to Jennifer and Jake.

Without looking, he was aware that she steadily sipped her drink until it was gone, then she put the glass down with a click that seemed to indicate some sort of decision.

'Jake, I want to tell you something about George. You've got the wrong idea, actually. George——'

'Don't, Jennifer.' He couldn't bear the thought of listening to her declare her love for another man. 'I don't really want to hear. I just don't like to see you—no, don't get your feathers up! I'm not going to lecture.'

She smiled. 'It sounded like the beginning of a lecture.'

'Maybe it was,' he admitted ruefully. 'Just a small lecture.' She relaxed, her shoulder touching his. He kept very still, saying, 'I *am* worried about you. George is your business. I've no right to interfere, but the sailing worries me.'

'Jake——' she turned towards him, her face only inches from his, her eyes dark and serious '—George has sailed all over—in the Caribbean, Tahiti. Even——'

'All right.' She wasn't his woman. She never would be, yet he had an almost irresistible desire to kiss her until she was trembling in his arms. Damn it! If she'd only let him have a chance! He couldn't keep the anger out of his voice as he said, 'Don't bother singing the man's praises.'

'George isn't a——'

He rode over her words hurriedly before she could say any more. 'Promise me one thing. No matter how experienced he is, these aren't waters to play with. Just look down there—no, forget about the damned aeroplane, but look at that water. We're just over the north end of the Charlottes. See, that's Graham Island below us.'

Her hair slid across his face as she nodded, looking where he pointed as he leaned across her and breathed in her scent. Was that her shampoo, or a particularly enticing perfume? She whispered, 'It looks beautiful, wild and——'

'There's Dixon Entrance,' he pointed, leaning across her until his other arm came curved around her back. For a second she seemed to lean back against his arm. His voice was husky as he went on, 'It's the stretch of water between the Charlottes and the Alaska Panhandle. You'll be crossing there from Ketchikan when you come south. It's big and damned near empty. You might not see another boat all day when you cross. It can be blue and beautiful and gentle, but——' his hand had gripped hers again, loosening when she winced '—but it can be nasty when it wants—black and stormy and deadly! You know my mother's people are from the islands?'

'Yes, I knew that.' She turned, her eyes looking into his, her lips parted, only inches from his. He had to concentrate on what he was saying.

'This is where they make their living, fishing these waters. My uncle and his two sons disappeared out here—the boat and the three of them. They were fishing, but it blew up a storm, a winter storm. A few years ago when the herring fishery was big, the fishermen used to fish through the worst of the winter storms; hiding out when they had to, fishing when they could. Uncle Daniel and his boys just disappeared. They were never heard from, never found. Some wreckage washed up on Rose Spit, but——'

Below them, the blue water was streaked with white from the wind.

'Jake——'

'I don't want to terrify you, just make you careful. I want you to promise you'll leave word every step of the way.'

He'd managed to get through her anger; she was watching him, saying earnestly, 'Leave word where?'

'With me. Phone me from Ketchikan—does George's boat have a radio-telephone?'

'Yes. George called me yesterday on it.'

'All right.' He sensed her slight movement away from him and dropped his arm, giving her more room. 'Phone me when you're leaving. Tell me your planned route, your expected arrival at the next port—Masset, will it be? On the Charlottes?'

'I'm not sure.' She was frowning, drawing herself back into that shell.

'Then find out, and call me. Promise?'

'All right,' she agreed, then her eyes met his briefly. 'Yes, I promise.'

'And when you get to Masset—if it is Masset—you'll call me again. Tell me you've arrived safely.'

She nodded, promising him, but drawing her reserve around her, avoiding his eyes and trying not to look out of the window as they banked to land.

'And—Jennifer?'

She refused to turn back, but he said it anyway. 'If you do change your mind, please don't hesitate to come back. Any time.'

When the plane landed, he stayed in his seat, watching her make her way up the aisle, her bag slung over one shoulder. She didn't look back, and he tried to tell himself it didn't matter.

He flew back to Vancouver on the same flight, earning a curious, laughing look from the stewardess.

Jennifer called the next day, ringing through when he was just coming out of his morning shower.

'Radio on line,' the operator announced.

'Jennifer? Where are you?' he stood, dripping on the carpet, listening to her voice all tangled up with a noise like a boat's engine.

'Ketchikan,' she said, sounding happy and excited. 'We're just leaving Ketchikan.'

And now they were overdue. She should have called him yesterday, reported their safe arrival on the Queen Charlottes. Just a day.

Where were they?

Jake swung away from the television, losing patience waiting for the weather broadcast, picking up his telephone and dialling the coastguard weather station.

'Why don't I take a taxi home?' Monica picked up her bag from the table, dropping in her cigarettes and snapping it closed.

Good idea, he almost said, quickly changing it to, 'I'll drive you.' How was he going to find Jennifer?

Monica threw him an angry glance and insisted, 'No, stay here. You're already dialling that number, whatever it is. I'll take a taxi home and we'll try this evening again when you're in better temper.'

He saw her clearly suddenly, saw the hurt in her eyes. 'Monica, I don't think——' he began, but stopped, realising he was in no state to do a decent job of telling her their affair was over. If he admitted the unpleasant truth to himself, Monica's main appeal had been a futile hope of getting a reaction out of Jennifer by dating her room-mate. Futile was right! Jennifer hadn't even blinked when he'd said he was probably going to marry Monica.

She was smiling when she left, but he knew she was angry, and she had reason. He should have gone after her, insisted on taking her home, kissed her and—and told her goodbye.

But Jennifer Winslow was somewhere out on the water, in a flimsy fibreglass sailboat, somewhere between Ketchikan and Masset.

And he was in Vancouver, almost helpless.

The man at Rescue Co-ordination Centre was very efficient about taking down the details of the *Lady Harriet*, overdue on a trip from Ketchikan, Alaska, to Masset on the Queen Charlotte Islands. Two people on board.

There was nothing more he could do from this far away. He dialled Hans and unknowingly interrupted a passionate interlude with a girl Hans had been pursuing for over a month. The girl got her blouse buttoned up and her coat on while Jake recited a long list of instructions to Hans, then hung up without saying where he was going, merely, 'I'll be back in a few days. I'll call you.'

As he had expected, the next flight to Sandspit airport on the Queen Charlottes was not fully booked.

CHAPTER FIVE

THEY had a tremendous sail across Dixon Entrance. The wind was on their beam, sending *Lady Harriet* scurrying across the whitecaps. Jenny spent most of the trip on deck, with the hood to her cruiser suit tied tightly around her face and her hands deep in the suit's pockets. Bundled up like that, only her face felt the spray as it flew over the boat.

It made her feel like an adventurer, a seafaring explorer, at one with the wind and the waves. When George leaned out of the cockpit and shouted something, Jenny pulled back her hood and leaned closer to listen.

'What did you say?' she shouted.

'Jenny, is that boat coming our way? I keep altering course, but he keeps heading towards me no matter what I do.'

The large, workmanlike fishing vessel loomed up on their port side. It passed behind them and circled to come up alongside on their windward side, keeping pace with them.

'He's blocking our wind,' shouted George. 'I hope he knows what he's doing. What does he want?'

Jenny went back out on deck in time to hear the loud-hailer from the fishing-boat.

'*Lady Harriet!* Can you turn on your radio?'

Jenny shook her head and shouted, 'No!'

'Wave both arms in the air if you have no radio!'

Jenny braced herself against a stay to keep from falling on the moving deck. She lifted both arms and waved at the fishing-boat.

'*Lady Harriet!*' boomed the fishing-boat, 'We're responding to a coastguard report that you are overdue at Masset. Do you want me to tell coastguard that you're OK and on your way into Masset?' Jenny signalled a 'yes' and the loud-hailer boomed, 'Roger! I'll relay that you are OK! Heading for Masset! I have *Julie II* calling me on channel sixteen. I'll relay your status to her as well.'

And with that the big fishing-boat pulled away in a long curve until it was heading east again. Jenny ducked into the cockpit.

George was smiling as if at a private joke. 'Someone seems to have declared us overdue.'

'Jake, of course.' Jenny made a futile attempt to wipe the rainwater off her face with a wet hand. 'He insisted on knowing when we'd be in Masset. Darn the man! He's had everyone looking for us!'

'We'd be glad of it if we were in trouble.'

'I guess. I suppose we should have planned more time to get to Masset.' Her hands were soaking wet. She rubbed them against the damp nylon of her suit.

George said, 'We couldn't be expected to know the weather would turn so foul. Of course, it wouldn't have mattered if the radio hadn't gone kaput.' George spun the wheel. 'You could have called someone and said you were OK, and your guardian angel would have relaxed. What's this about telling Julie we're all right? Who's Julie?'

'You've got me. I don't know what he was talking about. I thought he said he'd notify the *Julie II*. Another boat, maybe? Jake's started a terrible fuss over our being just three days late!'

'Don't knock it, Jenny. I wish I had someone to worry about me.' George turned away swiftly before Jenny could see her face. 'Take the wheel, would you? I'll make us some coffee.'

After two years, George still wasn't over Scott. In two years, would Jenny still be missing Jake? Ever since she'd left Vancouver she had felt as if a part of herself had been torn away. She kept turning to say things to him, tucking away small comments for the next time they were together.

Ever since she'd talked to him on the radio-phone from Ketchikan, she'd been looking forward to being able to call him again once they arrived in Masset. Somehow she had to find the will to break even that small contact. She couldn't deny that it made sense to have someone following their progress, someone who could press the panic button if they disappeared, but from now on it would have to be someone else. She had to get Jake right out of her life before she could succeed in forgetting him.

She was in love with him, but it wasn't the first time she'd been in love, so she knew it wouldn't last for ever. Once she stopped seeing Jake, stopped talking to him— then, eventually, she would stop wanting him, needing him.

What if they *had* been lovers? She would be dependent on Jake for her happiness...then, one day, there would be the moment when she reached for him with need...and found him gone.

It would happen to Monica one day. Maybe Jake *would* marry her, but eventually ...

She went back outside, taking the mug of coffee with her, standing in the wind and staring ahead at the Queen Charlotte Islands. *Lady Harriet* moved carefully as they approached Masset Inlet.

'We'll go round once,' suggested George as they approached the wharfs. 'If it looks easy to get in, we'll go in. If not, we'll steam back out and think it over before we try again.'

The whole thing went like a charm. Jenny got the lines in her hand and hovered at the side of the boat until it came close to the wharf, then she stepped off just as if she'd been doing it all her life.

Her smooth motions turned suddenly awkward and stiff as she sighted the big man in a floater jacket and captain's hat.

Jake! Here!

He stepped up and took the aft line from her. She let go of the line with a jerk, as if his hand had carried high voltage. She went forward to tie her line to the float while he tied the one at the back. George cut the engine and there was silence except for the sound of waves lapping against the wooden floats.

Jenny fiddled with the knot she was tying, her fingers numb and her heart thundering. At one point, out in the pounding waves, she'd had a brief fantasy that he would be here to meet them. She'd discarded it as nonsense.

Why was he here?

A grizzled fisherman in high boots and a sou'wester stomped up to Jake and said something. Jake stood up and pushed a lock of wet hair back under the captain's hat.

In the city, in city clothes, he looked like he belonged there—if you didn't look at his eyes and see the controlled hint of the untamed man; if you didn't look too closely at the harsh lines of his face.

Here, standing on a wharf on an island a few miles south of Alaska, talking to a tough-looking fisherman, Jake seemed to fit in perfectly.

The two men exchanged a few words that Jenny couldn't hear, then nodded at each other. Jake's nod was as abrupt as the fisherman's, but Jenny sensed somehow that they were friends.

The man stomped on, staring at Jenny as he passed, saying gruffly, 'See you made it all right. Crazy woman, tearing around in a plastic boat!'

Jake walked towards her. He wasn't smiling. She realised that she was. Her smile died nervously.

'Where in the devil have you been?'

His anger had the effect of calming her. She spoke confidently. 'We've been fine. Waiting for the weather. Sitting in a bay, perfectly safe.'

His feet were astride, his hands half clenched. She got the feeling that he wanted to shake her as he growled, 'Sam said you didn't have a radio?'

'Sam?'

'The captain of the fishing-boat that spotted you earlier today.'

She rubbed her hands against the wet fabric of her cruiser suit. 'The radio quit on our second day out.' She pulled on the string to untie her hood, but didn't push the hood back.

Jake snarled, 'And *George*, of course, couldn't manage to figure out what was wrong with it?'

'George didn't try. Radios aren't George's thing.'

'I'll bet they're not.' He glared at her, then said grudgingly, 'I'm glad to see you've got a cruiser suit on. At least George had the sense to get good gear for you. I was worried you'd catch your death in this cold wind.'

'It's not as if it were freezing!'

'Don't be an idiot, Jenny! Even in Campbell River you must have learned about hypothermia. You don't need to freeze to die of the cold!'

He looked so much like a stern father that she couldn't help laughing. 'Stop being such an alarmist, Jake! I know when to come in out of the cold.'

'Do you? I'm beginning to suspect you don't have any sense at all.'

She flared, 'If I'm such a pain in the neck, why do you bother with me? Why don't you just stay in Vancouver where it's warm and dry, and leave me to my fate?'

He looked past her, over her head at the other side of the harbour. When he answered, his voice had the exaggerated patience of a parent dealing with an aggravating small child. 'In the first place, Vancouver was pelting down rain when I left and I——' He stopped, shrugged, and finished lamely, 'And you may be a pain in the neck, but everything's been falling apart since you left.'

She threw her shoulders back and glared at him. 'Well, that's just too bad. I don't belong to Austin Media and I don't need you to follow after me, lecturing me on what to wear and what to do!'

Jake opened his mouth to shout a reply to her, then closed it abruptly. He was staring past her on to the deck of *Lady Harriet*.

George was standing there, tiny, dwarfed by the bulky yellow cruiser suit. Only George could manage to look glamorous in a Mustang cruiser suit! She had loosened her collar and pushed the hood back, letting her blonde curls tumble around her very feminine face, the one streak of grey at her temple.

Jenny couldn't help laughing at the look in Jake's eyes as George placed her hands on her yellow-clad hips and surveyed him before she said, 'Don't bother introducing me, Jenny. This has got to be Jake. Or do you know other men who would make a habit of shouting at you in strange ports?'

'Who the hell are you?' demanded Jake.

'George,' her cousin said smugly.

Jake almost stammered, 'G-George?'

The blonde head nodded. Jake stared at her, then turned to Jenny swiftly, furiously.

She said hurriedly, 'Jake, I never said George was a man!'

'Well, you sure as hell never said he—she was a girl!'

She caught herself before she stomped her foot, contenting herself with shouting back, 'It was none of your bloody business!'

'Jenny!' George had to raise her voice to get Jenny's attention. 'Are you coming inside for coffee? Or would you rather stay out here and fight?'

They looked at each other, slightly shamefaced, then Jenny said, 'All right, George, I'll behave. Jake, would you like to come in for a coffee?'

He followed them in. Jenny had the feeling that he was at a loss, didn't know what to say. He stooped to get through the companionway. The small boat wasn't designed for anyone as tall as Jake.

Inside, George stepped out of her cruiser suit. It was too large for her and slipped off easily.

Jenny's was tighter, damp from rain and spray. She unzipped the upper part and started to struggle out of the arms.

Jake grasped the arm and started pulling the damp nylon.

'I can get if off myself,' she protested, too aware of him towering over her, his arm half around her as he worked the suit down off her arms.

'Can you?' Damn him! He was laughing. She quit protesting and stood still as he peeled the suit down to her waist.

'You'd better change out of those clothes once we get this off.' He unsnapped the belt and bent to unzip the bottoms of the legs. 'You're all damp inside.'

She was a mess, her hair wild, her sweater damp and clinging too tightly to her body. Jake pushed the suit down around her legs.

'Lift your leg, Jennifer.'

She lifted, complaining, 'I feel like a two-year-old— "Stand still. Lift your leg. Here. I'll unzip your suit."'

Jake laughed and freed her left leg. 'Now lift the other one—there, you're free of it! Better hang it somewhere to dry. You don't look like a two-year-old.'

He stood back and let his eyes travel from her bare feet up, over her damp jeans and clinging sweater. She

flushed and shifted uncomfortably as his eyes lingered
on the curves of her breasts, then travelled up to her
face, her hair.

'What the devil have you done to your hair? You've
cut it!'

She lifted her hand and made a futile attempt to
smooth it back over her head.

'It looks——' He lifted his hand, stopping just short
of touching her hair.

'It looks what?' she asked defensively.

'Different. You don't look like Jennifer. This whole
thing——' He looked around, gestured at the small
saloon and galley, then back to Jenny. 'You, your
clothes, your hair. The way you're behaving here. It's
not like you.'

'Isn't it? Or is it that you don't know very much about
me? You never did.'

'You never let me,' he retorted, his eyes probing hers,
seeing her discomfort. 'Why?' he demanded.

Her heart was knocking against her ribs. She dropped
her eyes, afraid he was seeing too much. He mustn't
know how vulnerable she was to him. It had started that
first day, when she'd forced him to take her into his
business. She'd been attracted, known she wanted
nothing more than to work with this man, be close to
him. At the same time, she'd always known that if she
let him get close to her she would have no defences
against him.

'Why did you cut your hair?' he asked.

The hair; that was easy to answer. Relieved, she said,
'It was bothering me. It was in the way, always blowing
in the wind, tangling. George cut it.'

'George cut it?' He turned to look at George, who
had run a comb through her own hair and was looking
glamorous in blue jeans and an oversized sweater.
'George, your boyfriend?'

'George, her cousin,' said George, setting two steaming mugs down on the table. 'I cut it and dropped it overboard somewhere in Alaska.'

Jenny shifted uncomfortably. She wished she had a camera to shove into his hands, to distract him. 'Jake, stop staring at me like that.'

'Like what?'

'As if you were trying to probe my—as if I'm a subject for one of your films.'

'What will you do now, Jennifer?' he asked softly. 'You can't drop that curtain of glossy brown hair between yourself and the world.'

That was too close to home. She swallowed, and reached desperately for a change of subject. 'Would you please stop calling me Jennifer?'

'I've been calling you Jennifer for five years.'

'And I hate it. I've always hated being called Jennifer.' She looked up and found George looking at her curiously.

'Have you?' George asked. 'But didn't Lance always call you——'

Jenny said, sharply, *'George!'* and her cousin fell silent.

Jake lifted the mug slowly to his lips, watching her as he sipped the hot coffee. 'If you mind being called Jennifer, why didn't you tell me before?'

She laughed bitterly, 'Telling you never makes any difference.'

He took another big sip from the steaming cup. For a minute she thought she had gone too far, made him quietly, dangerously angry.

'Are you sure you've tried?' he asked conversationally. He didn't seem angry. 'You could always hit me over the head with it—like when you told me you quit. I got the message that time.'

She caught George's eye. Her cousin wasn't missing a word of this. And Jake had that look in his eye, as if he were searching for the meaning in a beautiful picture. She tried throwing a distraction in his path. 'I had to shout. You'd have walked out otherwise. You were hell bent to go to the North Shore—what was so important over on the North Shore that day?'

He said, 'Nothing that matters now,' and she had the feeling that he couldn't remember. Then he said briskly, 'If you go up to the hotel and tell the girl at the desk that you're Jake's friends, she'll show you where you can have a hot bath. I'll give you directions and you can go and have a long soak while I get someone to look at your radio.'

Jenny couldn't help feeling she should object to Jake's arranging their activities, just on general principle. But how could she? A hot bath sounded like heaven, and neither Jenny nor George knew the first thing about repairing radios.

She felt uneasy about walking into the hotel and demanding a bath, but George didn't hesitate.

'Jake told us to come,' she announced to the girl behind the counter.

'Oh, yes!' The girl put her pen down and picked up a key from the counter in front of her. 'You wanted a bath?'

A man crossing the lobby with his head down stopped, turned and stared at the two women who wanted a bath. Then he shrugged and walked on.

George had the first bath, then returned to the boat while Jenny had a long soak in the empty hotel suite. When she came out of the bathroom, she changed into clean jeans and a tailored shirt, bundling her old clothes into the small pack she had carried up to the hotel. Later, she and George would have to find a launderette.

She heard Jake's voice as she came down the stairs. He was leaning casually against the front desk, talking to the clerk. He looked so different out of city clothes, so hard and muscled and somehow uncontrollable.

He watched her coming down the stairs, his eyes taking in everything from her freshly scrubbed cheeks to the way her shirt clung to her still damp body.

'Feeling better?' he asked, his voice low.

'Much better!' She looked at the woman behind the desk. 'Thank you, that was lovely!'

Jake kept pace with her as they moved along the main street of Masset towards the docks.

Looking ahead, her hands pushed into her pockets as she walked, she asked, 'Why are you here, Jake?'

Deliberately misunderstanding, he said, 'I'm walking you to the docks.' Outside the Co-operative general store they passed two men standing together, deep in conversation. One lifted his hand in greeting to Jake.

'I'm not coming back to work for you, Jake.'

'Hi, Graham!' said Jake. 'How's the catch?'

'Jake! It's been years! Fishing's rotten!'

Jake nodded, said, 'Catch you later,' and guided Jenny off the edge of the pavement.

'Watch out!' he warned her as her foot went down on the uneven pavement, throwing her off balance.

She threw her arms out and found them clutching his chest. She pushed away, breathless, and said accusingly, 'You're here to get me back to work.'

He was silent until they were half a block away from the store, then he asked, 'How long do you want for your fling, Jennifer?'

'I asked you not to call me Jennifer,' she evaded.

'Yes, you did, didn't you? Lance used to call you Jennifer. Tell me about Lance.'

'*No!*' She stopped walking, her breath coming short, her voice trembling a little as she denied, 'Lance is nobody. Nothing.'

'Is he?' Jake stopped too, grasped her shoulders and turned her to face him. The lines of his face were deeper than usual. 'You know, somehow I don't believe that.'

She jerked away from him. '*Oh*, go dissect someone else's mind, will you? I've had enough of this! I'm going to find George. I'd appreciate it if you'd go off and amuse yourself somewhere else.'

'George is on *Julie II*. David and Glenda—*Julie II*'s owners—have invited you both for dinner. They sent me to fetch you.'

'Friends of yours?' she asked curiously.

'Old friends,' he agreed warmly.

Jenny could hear the sounds of George's guitar as she walked along the float with Jake. She moved quickly towards the music, away from Jake's probing.

'You didn't tell me it was a jam session.'

'I didn't know.' He grasped her arm to steady her as she stepped on to the fishing-boat. She pulled away, stumbling a little as Jake said, 'I didn't know they had a guitar.'

'That's George on the guitar. It's her favourite song. Hear her singing it?'

'For a tiny girl, she's got a big voice—hey, Jenny, stop running! Watch out!' His hand gripped, steering her clear of a big, jagged piece of metal on the back deck of the boat.

'What's that?'

'Fishing gear—it's all over the place, so watch your step. And don't run away so fast. I'm not going to hurt you.'

She was acting like an idiot, rushing across the cluttered deck of this boat to escape a few seconds alone with Jake. He must wonder what was getting into her. She took deep, slow breaths and turned around, facing him.

He was right behind her, one hand above his head, grasping one of the many pipes that ran over their heads. She said breathlessly, 'I had no idea there were so many strange pieces of metal on a fishing-boat.'

The music was coming through the closed door, but Jake and Jenny were alone out here. She could hear the sounds of the sea along with George's song.

Jake said huskily, 'You're really very beautiful,' and she realised in sudden panic that he meant to kiss her.

'I'm not,' she whispered, staring wide-eyed as his lips approached hers.

It was the softest kiss, a whisper of his skin against hers, a warm movement that left her trembling, unable to move away as her eyes were pulled into a long, deep contact with his.

'What are you afraid of?' he asked softly.

'Nothing,' she lied, her eyes pulling away. She shivered, hugging herself. 'It's cold, isn't it? Shall we go in?'

'We may as well,' he said wryly, calling out, 'Permission to board!'

A heavily accented Scots voice from inside replied, 'Come ahead, Jake!'

The inside of this fishing-boat was crammed with people. The big voice belonged to a red-headed man in the corner.

'There you are! Come in! Come in! You're Jennifer? We've been worried about you and George these last few days—thought George was a man, in fact!' The blue eyes glinted with humour. 'Glad to see you here safe. This is Glenda, my wife!' He gestured to a heavy-set woman squeezed in at his side. 'Come in, girl! Come to the fire! Glenda, get a drink for them.'

Glenda wasn't a Scot. If anything, her voice had an American accent. 'You'll have your usual, Jake? What about you, Jennifer? Coffee? Tea? Beer? We're having dinner in a few minutes—it's just about done.' She gestured to an oil stove on the far side of the cabin, near where George and a teenage boy were bent over George's guitar. 'That's my son, Gerry. He's in seventh heaven, learning to play guitar. What will you have to drink, Jennifer?'

'Call me Jenny, please. I'll have whatever George had.'

That was beer. Jenny sipped it as she listened to Jake and David MacDougal catching up on each other's lives. She learned that fishing had been good for David this year, and that another good year would assure their son's university education.

When Glenda moved into the galley, Jenny stepped around the men to join her, helping to hand out steaming bowls of clam chowder and fresh biscuits.

There wasn't room for them all at the small table. They ate sitting around the oil stove, holding their bowls in their hands, talking about fishing and music and the Queen Charlotte mining town that had just been bull-dozed into the ground.

The boy, Gerry, said he hoped he'd get a guitar for Christmas.

'He's already spoiled,' said David with a grin. 'He's our only child, and I think he gets everything he wants too easily.'

George smiled at Gerry. 'You won't get too much support for that notion from us. Jenny and I are both only children.'

So was Jake, although he didn't say so. He was leaning back in the corner of the settee, watching them all as if he were composing a shot for his camera.

She didn't think he was listening until he asked, 'Were you spoiled, Jennifer?'

'Of course,' she agreed.

George was back at her guitar, but her fingers fell silent and she said, quietly and directly to Jake, 'Don't let her fool you. Jenny never saw enough of her parents to get spoiled. My aunt and uncle spent their lives working their way around the world. They left Jenny behind.'

Jake's eyes moved from George to Jenny, probing. Jenny got up, taking his bowl out of his hand and moving over to the galley, her voice cold as she denied, 'George is exaggerating. Glenda, can I help with those dishes?'

Glenda reached for a dish-towel. 'I'd be a fool to refuse that offer. If we get them out of the way, we'll have more room.'

Someone from another boat heard the music and came along with an accordion, making even more music—and dancing. Jenny wouldn't have thought there was room on board *Julie II* for anything more than quiet conversation, but one couple managed to dance on the wheel-house floor, though they did have to be careful.

The moon came out. The rain stopped. The musicians moved outside with the dancers. Jenny found herself outside on the wharf, swinging on David MacDougal's arm to a polka.

Then there was Jake, taking her in his arms and moving her smoothly over the planks to the strains of a haunting waltz.

'Enjoying yourself?' he asked as he swept her gently across the wharf.

'Yes,' she admitted, tipping her head back to look at his face in the moonlight. 'But I'm exhausted! I thought David would spin us into the water with that polka.'

'Relax,' he told her. 'I'll do the work. Close your eyes.'

She shook her head, still smiling, but half-serious as she said, 'I don't dare. If I close my eyes, where will you take me?'

'Trust me,' he suggested, and in the midst of the darkness and the music, it almost seemed that she could.

It was so easy to sway in his arms, her eyes closed, letting him guide their steps. When his hands slid to her wrists, she let him guide her arms, slipping them both around his neck and giving herself up to the night.

The music stopped momentarily as George and the man with the accordion consulted on their next number. Jenny opened her eyes and looked back at George sitting on the gunwale of the fishing-boat.

The music began again, disjointed at first, then coming together into a popular Western tune. Jake kept his arms around her waist.

Jenny twisted around and asked, 'Won't somebody complain about the noise?'

'Not likely. I think they're all here.' The party had grown as the evening went on, people joining them in ones and twos. The MacDougals' teenage son was still firmly attached to George. Jenny closed her eyes again as Jake gathered her close to move with the music. She drifted on a tide of fantasy until Jake said, 'I see George is wearing a wedding ring. Where's Mr George?'

George was having fun tonight, but Jenny knew the sadness would still be there if she looked deep into her cousin's eyes. 'He died.'

'Recently?' asked Jake.

'Two years ago.'

He swept her in a sudden turn, avoiding a collision with David and Glenda.

'Having a good time?' shouted David. Jenny nodded.

Above her head, Jake's voice asked, 'Was his name Lance?'

Startled, she said, 'Scott. His name was Scott. Lance was——' She broke off, tried desperately to think of a change of subject that would divert him.

They bumped into another couple. Jake steered her away from the light and the music. She pulled back out of his arms, feeling the cool night air through her blouse.

He said, 'I was just trying to figure something out.'

'Jumping to conclusions again, Jake?' she accused him, forcing the anger, hoping to divert his enquiry into her past. 'What is it now? You've got me having an affair with George's husband?'

'Take it easy,' he said, drawing her back towards him, his voice low and persuasive. 'I didn't mean anything by that. I——'

'*You did!*' She shook his hands away, but they wouldn't leave her arms.

'I wasn't accusing you of anything. I'm just trying to figure you out and——' He shrugged, and he looked strangely at a loss for words.

'Why?' she asked with a tinge of desperation in her voice. 'Why do you have to figure me out?'

He shook his head, his hands moving along her arms, palms brushing against her skin. 'I don't know,' he admitted, drawing her closer, kissing her with a sudden, rough gentleness, not giving her time to respond or push away before his hands dropped and she was standing alone, staring at him, finding herself aching for his touch.

'Jake,' she whispered, the music drowning her words. 'Please don't——'

He was waiting for her to finish, but she shrugged and turned away. 'Goodnight, Jake. I'm tired.'

He didn't try to stop her, but his deep voice followed her. 'Jennifer Winslow, you intrigue the hell out of me!'

CHAPTER SIX

JENNY shifted in her bunk, trying to recapture the images of a dream she wasn't ready to leave. Sounds, low but insistent, had been working their way into her consciousness for some time.

The drone of an engine, suddenly louder, then receding. The roar of a truck, a horn honking: signs of daytime, of civilisation.

And closer, the steady intrusion of George's voice. And Jake's.

'It's risky,' Jake was saying to George, then other words she couldn't hear. Eyes closed, ears open, she caught something about spring tides ... sure to wait ... even the pilot advises local knowledge.

' ... a great idea!' That was George's voice.

Jake and George plotting—what? If Jake convinced George that Jenny was better off back at work, her cousin was capable of waging an irresistible campaign. Jenny tried to remember even once when she had managed to hold out against a determined George.

Or a determined Jake. She'd succeeded in quitting, leaving Vancouver against his wishes. But he was here, now, still fighting that battle.

'What are you two plotting?' she demanded a moment later as she came out of her cabin.

Jake was sitting across the table from George. Was he staying with David and Glenda aboard the *Julie II*? If so, the fishing-boat must be equipped with a shower. His hair was still damp, just beginning to wave over his forehead. He pushed it back as he looked up from the book in front of him. He smiled, seeing Jenny, but she saw the swift glance he exchanged with George.

'We're plotting your safe passage.' He was smiling, but his eyes were telling her this was no joke. 'Since you insist on having this fling, I'm trying to do what I can to keep you two maniacs from being shipwrecked on an unfriendly rock.'

'Fling?' She poured herself a cup of coffee from the pot on the stove, thinking hard. He was talking sailing, but he had some plan to get her back in his studio, back to being Jenny-in-the-back-room, watching him with Monica. She met his eyes deliberately, held them as she walked across to the table.

She didn't sit down. Standing, she had the advantage of height over him. Her heart was pounding, but she managed to make her voice hard and cold as she said, 'I think it's time we got something straight.'

His eyes sparkled dangerously, challenging her. She put her cup down, pushed her hands into her jeans' pockets and hunched her shoulders. She was losing her cool and her voice showed it as she said aggressively, 'This nice, social visit isn't fooling anybody, Jake! You didn't come to give advice, or to have a morning cup of coffee with us. You came to bring me back to Vancouver.'

Her words rang through the little boat, but he didn't answer. He was waiting.

'Isn't that right?' she demanded.

'Yes,' he agreed, his voice refusing to give anything away.

'Jake, I'm not on holidays. If you're thinking that I'll be back to finish the Madison series, or any other work, *you're wrong*! This isn't just a fling. I've quit! I won't be back! I'm not your affair any more.'

Affair.

The word hung between them. There had never been an affair, but for just a moment his eyes were heated with intimate knowledge of her. She felt her face growing hot. She followed his glance, down over the curve of her breasts, the swell of her hips. As if he could see through the light summer fabric.

She picked her cup up, turning it in her hands, meeting George's eyes and finding no help there, only a warm curiosity.

The heat drained out of Jake's eyes. His voice was casual, as if she were a chance acquaintance. 'George says you're planning to go down the west coast of Graham Island. Do you know that most of the inlets out there are uncharted?'

He hadn't listened to a word she had said!

'Yes,' said Jenny, her voice taking on a flat, aggressive tone that he'd never heard before. 'We don't go into any bays unless we have good charts. We're not totally inexperienced.'

Their eyes met again, sparks flaring between them as Jake asked, 'And you're planning to visit Queen Charlotte City?'

'*Yes!*' She glared at him.

George was frowning. 'I don't know, Jenny. Jake just read the Pacific Pilot book to me—I didn't realise that the narrows west of Queen Charlotte were that hazardous. I did want to go in, but maybe we should reconsider.'

Jake pushed the book across to her, his finger jabbing at the paragraph on Skidegate Narrows. 'Read it, Jennifer!'

It wasn't cheerful reading. The passage was shallow, tortuous, and subject to treacherous currents.

'You're saying we shouldn't go through?' Jenny pushed the Pilot book back to him. Just what was he up to?

'Not without a guide,' he said, his eyes moving swiftly to George and back again.

Jenny reached over and slammed the book shut. 'You two have already worked this out!'

George said quickly, trying to pacify Jenny, 'Jake volunteered to guide us.'

Jenny glared at Jake. 'Why? Getting us through the narrows isn't going to help you get me back to work.'

Jake shrugged. She demanded, 'Or is it just another one of your attempts to run my life?'

'I guess that's it,' he agreed. George let out a soft noise that might have been a giggle.

Jenny ignored her, anger in her voice as she demanded. 'The book—this book says the narrows shouldn't be navigated without intimate local knowledge. Do you have intimate local knowledge?'

'I know the way through.' He was smiling, knowing she wanted him to lose that cool control, to be goaded into anger. What was getting into her? Looking for fights with Jake was asking for trouble.

She took refuge in the details of navigation. 'You said the passage was well marked?'

'It is,' he agreed with a slight smile. 'And there's at least one wreck visible on shore.'

Jenny paused, knowing he had her on this one. George was looking on Jake with approval, evidently glad of the offer of guidance. There wasn't much she could do about it. Jake would be guiding them, but she didn't have to like it.

She sat down beside George, directly facing Jake. 'How come you're so available to help us, Jake? How are you managing time to follow us around the Pacific? Don't you have to go back to work?'

He picked up his own cup and sipped before he answered. Today he was wearing a heavy-knit Indian sweater that carried a stylised raven design. He looked like one of the locals. She tried to close her eyes and imagine him back in the city. He was less dangerous there, easier to handle—if Jake could ever be described as easy to handle!

'I'll go back to Vancouver this afternoon on the jet from Sandspit,' he told her. 'I've only been away three days—a weekend's work will catch it up.'

'Then you don't need me, do you? If it only takes a couple of days to catch up.'

His eyes flashed, but his voice was neutral. 'I'll fly back next Wednesday. George has my aunt's telephone number—I have an aunt living in Queen Charlotte. When you get to the west side of the narrows, you can call me——'

'Call you? How?'

'Radio-telephone. Yours is working now— David fixed it. A loose wire.'

'Oh. So I'll call.' She glared at him, but it made no impression at all. 'I suppose there's no point telling you to get out of my life?'

'No point at all,' he agreed mildly, refusing to rise to her anger. His smile infuriated her.

'And what about your work?' she demanded again. 'A week here, a week there. Unless Austin Media has changed, it's not enough. There're still two episodes in the Great Hamburger Caper to be filmed, aren't there? And the Eglinton film.'

'Only one hamburger episode. I've managed to finish one, and I've left Hans working on the last one—what did you say?'

'Nothing.' Giving her opinion of Hans wasn't going to get either of them anywhere.

She took her cup to the sink as Jake informed her, 'I thought I'd take you sightseeing this morning.'

She wanted to see his islands, but ... She stared down at the cup in her hands, admitting that she'd missed him terribly ever since she had got off that jet in Ketchikan. Now, knowing he would be meeting them again in a few days, she felt excitement and anticipation growing inside herself.

Was she insane? Jake was going back to Vancouver meanwhile. He would return to her directly from Monica. God, poor Monica! Jake was marrying her, yet only moments ago his eyes had been hot with desire as they roved over Jenny.

If she were to answer his desire with her own, meet his eyes honestly and boldly——

No! She wasn't going to be Jake's next girl, a temporary mistress, left lonely and desperate when the affair was over.

But what if she did? Would he still marry Monica? Or wouldn't it matter that he had been unfaithful to his promised bride?

Her eyes shifted back to him. He'd been watching her, trying to see her thoughts. She recovered quickly, asking, 'What about George? Are you taking us both sightseeing?'

George said, 'I'm busy, giving guitar lessons to Gerry. He sings, and he'd like to play. You could join us if you like, Jenny.'

'Not me!' The two cousins laughed together and Jenny's voice was bright and superficial as she explained to Jake, 'I'm the girl they threw out of the church choir.'

He smiled and the tension was gone. She felt the warmth flowing through her body, her lips curving in response to his as he said, 'I thought you had a blameless past. What did you do to get tossed out of the choir?'

'I sang,' she admitted, grinning.

George said, 'They didn't really throw her out.'

Jenny agreed, 'No, but I got the message when the bishop came to town and the choirmaster asked me just to move my lips, not make any noise. I know my limits. I'll stick to singing in the shower when no one else is around. If it's a choice between a jam session and a sightseeing tour, I'd better take the tour.'

The deck shifted under their feet as they left. Jake asked, 'What happened after the bishop?'

'I know when I'm not wanted. I just went away and didn't come back.'

He said softly, 'That's a bad habit of yours, running away instead of fighting back.'

A speedboat roared past, setting the larger boats swaying on its wake. Jenny stepped off *Lady Harriet*. Jake stepped down behind her. There was no one else in sight, only the boats tied to either side of the float.

Fighting back was dangerous. She knew better than to stand up and ask to be rejected.

'It's safer,' she said finally, not looking at him.

His hand came down on her shoulder, turning her towards him. It was very quiet. The water was still, his eyes deep and waiting. 'Is safety important to you?'

If she touched him, he would take her in his arms. She closed her eyes briefly, remembering when she had first started working for Jake.

He had seemed deeply involved with a dark-haired woman named Elissa. Jenny had seen them dancing once, Jake's arms around her, his eyes warm with desire as they looked down. Then, suddenly, Jake wasn't seeing her any more. She was gone, with no sign of regret on Jake's side.

When he'd asked Jenny to dinner, his eyes had held the same look he'd had for the other woman. Her lips had parted, almost saying yes before she got her refusal out. Jenny wasn't about to become the next one.

Keep it cool. Don't get involved deeper than you can handle if it ends. She'd learned the rules, and Jake was too dangerous to play with. Yet working with him, beside him every day, she had learned the joys of sharing his creations, of becoming indispensable to him.

Now, five years later, he was waiting for an answer. 'Safety? Yes, that's what's important.' As she walked beside him, not touching, she could still feel the imprint of his hand on her shoulder.

He probed, 'But you've left your job, gone off on to the ocean on a small boat—where's safety there?'

'There are different kinds of safety,' she said ambiguously. Safety was in getting away from Jake, keeping herself independent, not needing anyone else.

Softly, he asked, 'What is it you're running from this time?'

'I'm not running!'

'Aren't you?' He stopped, holding a hand out and catching her fingers in his. 'I don't know why, but I do think you're running from something. If it's dissatisfaction with your job, with me——' he gripped her hand tightly in a brief spasm '—if that's it, you could have asserted yourself, told me—wouldn't that have been easier than running?'

'It's easy enough for you to say that, but you're a dynamo, Jake. You do things the way you want. Fighting you takes more energy than I've got.'

He shook his head, keeping hold of her hand when she tugged to get it free. 'I don't believe that. You always avoid arguments.' He laughed, said, 'At least, you did until a few days ago. Why is that, Jenny? Because you can't argue without getting involved?'

He was too close, too curious. She jerked free, gripped the rail and kept her eyes down as she went up the steep ramp to the car park. 'Where are you taking me?'

And why was she going with him?

'Tow Hill—nice scenery, a beach, campsite in the wilderness—a picnic lunch, too. Glenda packed a basket for us. It's in the truck—David loaned me his truck.'

They were at the top of the ramp. She looked at him, tall and lean and aggressive. He was always restless, always moving, and she said, 'You mean, you're just going to laze about on a beach?'

He grinned down at her. 'That's right.'

'A whole morning with no rushing about, no camera, no traumatic events—that can't be the Jake I know.'

'But you don't know it all, do you?'

No, she didn't. Seated behind the wheel of an old, workmanlike truck, Jake didn't look like a man who owned a fast sports car.

Just seeing him again sent her pulses racing. Letting him show her his beloved islands wasn't going to make Jenny's bid for freedom any easier. If she didn't watch herself, he could talk her right back into his studio, right back where she'd been two weeks ago.

Remember Monica, she taunted herself as she pretended to watch the trees and the ocean.

When the silence became uncomfortable, she asked, 'Are you going to take me driving on the beach? You never did tell me if you were one of those teenagers who got cars stuck out on the sand when the tide came in. I saw the beach as we came in—it looks like it goes on for ever.'

'It does. As for my past, around here, you might hear a few tales of my wilder days. Mostly I was kept busy in my summers. I only came to the Charlottes for the summers, you know. To visit my mother's people.'

'I've been reading about the Haida.'

'Of course you have,' he said with a smile.

'You're laughing at me!'

He threw her a warm glance. 'Only a little. You always do your research. You probably know more facts about the Haida people than I do.'

'Is it true that all Haida are either ravens or eagles?' He nodded and she asked, 'Which was your mother?'

'A raven.'

'That makes you a raven, too, doesn't it? Yes, of course. That's why your sweater has the raven design on it. And that silver chain you wear—that's a raven design, too?'

'Yes,' he agreed, but she thought he looked more like an eagle, or even a hawk.

'And your aunt—the girl at the hotel called her a Haida princess. Your mother must have been a princess, too. That makes you royalty, doesn't it?'

Jake laughed, his hand tossing the unruly lock of black hair back. 'Violet's not a princess—that's white man's myth. She and my mother were daughters to a chief, but Haida don't have princesses. Here, we'll park under these trees and walk. What are you wearing for shoes? Good. They'll do for the rocks, and you can take them off on the beach.'

There was another vehicle parked under the trees, although Jenny saw no sign of its owners.

'Probably hiking up Tow Hill,' suggested Jake, gesturing to the large hill that rose from the shore. He watched her taking in their surroundings, her short curls blowing around her head in the wind.

'I think I like your hair like that,' he said, surprising himself. 'It makes you look—here, watch out for that hole! There are beavers here, I think. See that tree? It's been felled by a beaver not long ago.'

She looked up at him as he caught her arm, waiting for him to finish his statement about her hair. Instead, he said, 'We'll go this way first, out on the rocks. Then we'll come back and find a spot on the beach for our picnic.'

The ocean stretched to the mountains of Alaska. Off to their right, a sandy beach extended as far as they could see.

She followed him along a path, over rocks, finally coming to rest on granite that the ocean had worn into a gentle curve.

They sat, quietly watching as the green, turbulent water crashed up against the rocks below. When she looked, she found Jake's eyes on her, a lazy smile in their depths.

'Are you plotting something?' she asked warily, then waved his answer away. 'No, don't tell me. I'm enjoying this too much. Don't spoil it.'

'Nice, isn't it?'

'Perfect,' she agreed. 'How long is it since you've been here?'

He looked out over the wild shoreline, memories in his eyes as he reminded her, 'Last year I came for my grandfather's funeral.'

'But how long since you've really taken the time to come back and look at it all? I've never seen you so relaxed as you are right now.'

He shrugged, smiling wryly. 'The sickness of cities, Jenny. I always seem to be in a hurry—but you can't appreciate the islands properly when you're hurrying. It's years since I really took time to visit these islands properly. This is another world, a different time-zone— There, look behind you! The blowhole is about to go!'

Jenny turned quickly, startled by the roar as a huge geyser of water shot up from the rocks in a noisy, spectacular display of nature ... then subsided as if it had never been. 'It's a hole in the rocks,' Jake explained. 'When the tide is just right, and the waves the right size, water surges into the hole from below and shoots up like that. I was hoping we'd get a chance to see it today.'

'This is the real Jake,' she decided aloud, watching his pleasure, feeling his oneness with these wild surroundings. 'You're a reflection of all this, aren't you?'

'Am I?' He glanced back, smiling whimsically. 'How's that?'

'The artist and the fisherman, the Haida and the white man. You're all of them, more than anyone else. You should do this, Jake, get it down on film.'

'Tow Hill?' His black brows shot up as he gestured to the hill rising behind them.

'All of it. Capture the atmosphere of this place. What's island time? Glenda said everyone out here runs on island time.'

He made a broad gesture, taking in the water, the beach, the ancient forest behind. 'Can't you feel it?

People who live on islands have a special relationship with their environment. Time moves slower, hasn't the same meaning as it does to mainlanders.'

He looked out over the water again, smiling. 'I'd love to put it all down on film, but I'd get carried away, you know. To me, it's all beautiful.'

She sat up straight, touched his arm and found her fingers lingering. 'I was listening to you and David last night, Jake. It's such a mix—Haida villages with totem poles and satellite dishes for television. Fishermen with old nets and new electronic equipment. Jets to Vancouver, mining towns, logging towns, old-style homestead farms. And politics, for heaven's sake! Here we are in the middle of nowhere, at the edge of the ocean, sixty miles from the mainland, and these islands are in the midst of a political explosion with land claims and environment protection protests!'

'We're a political people. I guess we always have been. A hundred years ago we were terrorising the mainland, taking slaves. But, Jennifer——' His eyes reflected an odd uncertainty. 'Jenny, I wouldn't know where to start. It takes an outsider to see all that. Or someone like you. You always see the whole.'

'And you see the beautiful pictures,' she said softly, 'but you don't step back and see it all together.'

He caught her hand, admitting, 'I know that, but it never mattered. Not while I had you to keep everything in balance.'

'What do you mean?' she whispered, as her heart stopped.

'You know what I mean.' He kept her eyes on their linked hands, his voice low. 'Without you stopping me, I tend to go off collecting a meaningless jumble of pictures—beautiful pictures, granted, but you're the one who pulls it all together, gives it meaning.' His voice dropped to a whisper. 'I need you back, Jennifer.'

'Jake, I——' She stared down at their hands. His was large and brown, engulfing her small white fingers. She wanted to turn her hand in his and let her fingers curl, clinging to his.

She wished she could go back and work with him, but she mustn't. Something was happening to the barrier she had always kept between them. She couldn't trust herself any more. She might reach out for him, clinging, asking for whatever he would give her.

'Will you work on it with me, Jennifer—Jenny?' he corrected himself, his eagerness for the project revealed in the sudden tension of his body. 'I'll shoot the pictures, you direct it, put it together.'

She stood up on shaky legs, pulled her hand away to brush imaginary dust from her jeans. She tossed her hair back and wished she hadn't got George to cut it, wished she could drop a barrier between them by bending her neck forward.

Briskly, she said, 'Lunch on the beach, you said, and I'm hungry. I didn't have breakfast. Just that cup of coffee.'

He got up slowly, his lips parted on words he couldn't seem to say. Then he shrugged and gestured for her to lead the way back.

They walked back through the campground, passing a family with two young children. The children were busily and inefficiently pitching a tent under the trees.

'We saw a bear,' said the boy, 'but it ran away.'

'Just as well,' said Jake with a laugh, catching Jenny's hand to lead her past the tent.

The beautiful, hard-packed sand stretched on as far as Jenny could see. Behind them, she could hear the sound of the children laughing. Ahead, there was only the surf on the hard sand.

'Taking off your shoes?' Jake asked, bending to unlace his.

'Of course!' She slipped off her shoes and moved off, down the slow slope of the beach.

Long waves rushed across the sand, churning froth in an uneven, white line. Jenny walked along the edge of the water, letting the occasional wave swirl around her ankles.

'You've changed.' His voice followed her, low and throbbing in her ears. 'You don't look like a Jennifer now, or act like one.'

The sun was bright, its heat in sharp contrast to the cold water around her ankles. She bent down to roll up her jeans, asking curiously, 'What does a Jennifer act like?'

'Restrained, contained.' He gestured to her hair as he said, 'Long, brown hair dropping across her face, hiding the real woman from any invaders. Jenny is a different girl. Barefoot and elusive, but——' he grinned '—stubborn.'

She couldn't help smiling, although she recognised that he was trying to assess her new behaviour, to manoeuvre her into doing what he wanted. 'Maybe I got tired of doing everything the way you want it.'

'Everything?' he challenged, his eyes losing their coolness. 'Are you sure you know what it is that I want?' As she turned away in confusion, his voice changed, became brisk and almost impersonal. 'Jenny, are you going to help me with this film?'

She watched a puffy, white cloud moving slowly towards the west. She should say a direct 'no,' but she found herself evading, 'You don't need me to do it. They're your islands. It's your story.'

'I won't do it without you.' He dug his toe into the sand, making a hole that quickly filled with water. 'If we did it together, I think we might make another award winner.'

An award winner? Was that the most important thing to him?

Jenny had watched the women come and go, and they never really touched him the way a new idea did, a chance to take his camera and create a mood on film. He'd told her he was going to marry Monica, but right now Monica meant nothing compared to the excitement of a new film.

'No, Jake. If you do this film, you're doing it alone.' She fought down sadness at the knowledge that she couldn't work with him again, couldn't share the excitement.

There was a white sail on the horizon, someone tacking far north of the point at Rose Spit to clear the concealed sand bar.

'If you change your mind . . .' His voice trailed off.

'I'll let you know,' she said briskly, refusing to get caught in the melancholy that was threatening her. He was standing still, his hands in his pockets, his feet bare beneath a rolled-up pair of denim jeans. She found herself wondering aloud, 'What kind of a boy were you? Did you run barefoot on these beaches?'

'Sometimes. Most summers I worked on my uncle's fishing-boat. What about you? How did you spend your summers?'

She shrugged. 'In Campbell River. Getting into trouble with George, mostly.'

'You didn't go on holidays? With your parents?'

'No,' she said flatly. He was waiting for more, so she found herself saying, 'Dad kept taking jobs in places like South America and Africa. They loved moving, seeing new places, but they thought I should have a stable home. I stayed with George and her mother when they were out of the country. When they came home, it usually wasn't for long.'

'You were a lonely child,' he realised, his eyes seeing more than she wanted. She shrugged uncomfortably.

'Come on, Jake. I didn't suffer. I had a home. Aunt Georgina—George's mother—wasn't a dragon. She was a nice lady. She was widowed, and I'm sure we made

her life into chaos at times, but she didn't often complain—— My ankles are starting to hurt from the cold
water!' she complained, moving abruptly out of the path
of the waves and away from him.

He followed. They walked away from the water. Jake
took her hand to help her over a log, then failed to re-
lease it when they were back on level ground.

He said, 'I'm just beginning to realise how isolated
you were. You've always seemed so self-sufficient, as if
you didn't want anyone close—but you learned that,
didn't you? With your parents gone most of the time.'

'I——' She shook her head, confused by his penetrating insight into her childhood. 'No, there was always
George. She was older, but we were usually
together…until she got married—you don't want to hear
all this.' Jenny tugged at her hand, but he held it firmly.

He pulled her hand through his arm so that she was
walking close against him, their shoulders and hips
touching as they moved along the sand. 'What you really
mean is that you don't want to share it with me. When
did George get married?'

Off guard, she answered, 'I was sixteen, just turning
seventeen.' She remembered that summer, the warm
happiness that had grown in George's eyes as the weeks
passed. 'It was a big romance—George and Scott—very
sudden. Aunt Georgina was really upset about it, because
Scott was so much older. But George was so happy, and
no one could stop her. Aunt Georgina wouldn't consent,
so in the end they eloped.'

'And then?'

Jake's voice hardly disturbed the thread of Jenny's
memory. 'I don't know. I didn't see much of her after
that. They lived in Vancouver, and I went to the
University of Victoria.'

He was silent, thinking. With his probing eyes, he
might easily see far too much. She said swiftly, defensively, 'That doesn't tell you anything about me.'

But he'd already seen more than her words. 'You worked hard, didn't you?'

'Lots of people work hard at university.'

'Not much social life?' he guessed. 'And once you came to work for me—there hasn't been anyone. Boyfriends, but not anyone who mattered. Not since Lance.'

Her fingers tensed in a spasm on his arm. How had she got into this? Talking to Jake about her past, for heaven's sake! 'You promised me lunch,' she evaded desperately, 'and I'm still hungry. I think——'

'It was Lance, wasn't it? The man who called you Jennifer?'

He wasn't going to let her get away, wasn't going to stop asking until she answered. His eyes were watching, waiting.

Somehow, through all the years she worked for him, she'd managed to avoid answering questions like this. She didn't answer now, or even nod, but he seemed to read the story in her face, because his voice softened and he asked, 'When was Lance?'

She shrugged, making her voice casual, wishing the lump would go away, the tears stop threatening. 'I met him when George was dating Scott. We went out together.'

'And then George got married.' He was filling in the blanks as if he had been there, watching. 'You were alone then, weren't you? No parents, no George. And you weren't close to your aunt.'

She jerked her arm away, pushing both hands through her short, soft hair. 'Oh, God! I—— *Why are we doing this?* I don't want to talk about him. I don't want to think about him.'

'You're thinking about him all the time,' Jake accused. 'You never forget. You opened up once, to Lance, and you got hurt. So you're keeping the memory warm, making sure you never let anyone else close enough to get a knife in you again.'

'*Stop it!* I don't—— You're making a big thing of this. It was only a teenage romance!'

The blue sky and the sand, the ocean roaring over the sand in long, unstoppable surges. And Jake, prying, watching, finding the weak places in her. She said desperately, 'You should have brought a camera today. You could have got some terrific shots of this beach.'

But he wasn't being distracted. He accused softly, 'Hiding again, Jennifer? Running away from yourself? Don't you think it's time you talked about it all? You never have, have you?'

She was silent, but he was putting the pieces together. 'George didn't know—it was obvious when she mentioned his name last night that she had no idea he meant so much to you.'

'He doesn't,' she lied weakly.

'Then why not talk about him?'

She muttered, 'You're like a dog with a bone. You won't stop. What do you want me to say?' She avoided his eyes, then said in a rush, 'I fell in love with him. He was older, very impressive to a girl my age. We had an affair. Then he left. It's an old story. I was seventeen and I cried a lot. Now I'm twenty-eight and it's ancient history.'

Jake brushed gently at her cheek, as if he were wiping tears away. 'Why did he leave?'

She said tonelessly, 'Because I told him I was pregnant.'

She felt his shock in the moment of silence before he asked, 'And were you?'

Jake was watching her as if her old hurts mattered to him and she found herself talking, unable to stop.

'He wasn't local. He was a salesman, travelling around the northern part of Vancouver Island. I was always waiting for the next time he came—I was obsessed, I think. I was so lonely after George got married. I didn't really understand what was happening to me, but Lance seemed like the answer to my dreams.' She laughed bitterly. 'Well, I was pretty young, and I guess I thought a man of my own would make everything right.' She took a shallow, ragged breath. 'Lance said he loved me. That seemed to be all that mattered. I——We——He was there, and gone again, and I never seemed to know for sure when I'd see him again.

'I was full of dreams. I kept hoping I'd find I was expecting his child. It wasn't likely. He'd made sure I was on the Pill. But I kept dreaming weddings and babies and happy-ever-after. One night we were sitting in his car, parked near the ocean——' She closed her eyes, saw angry clouds hanging low over the stormy sea, pain surging up inside her at the memories. 'I didn't even know I was going to say it until the words came out ... I told him I was pregnant.'

She stood in the sand, shivering, unable to get her face into a mask. Jake, staring at her intently, could see everything. He reached out slowly, took her shoulders in his hands, drew her down beside him, sitting in the sand.

'What happened then?' he asked, and his dark, intense face drowned out everything else as he put his arms around her and drew her into his warmth.

'Nothing. I just—I never saw him again. I would have written, making more of a fool of myself, but he'd never given me an address to write to. I guess he was married, but I never thought of that—not at first. I kept waiting for him to call.' She shrugged. 'After a while, I stopped waiting.'

His arms were far too strong to fight, and his heat was soaking into her. She let herself relax, too weak to struggle.

Jake said, thoughtfully, 'And you never let anyone that close again?'

'You're the first person I've ever told about Lance,' she admitted.

He nodded, half smiling with a gentle teasing. 'How does it feel?'

'Odd,' she admitted. 'I hadn't realised—— I'm not even sure what he looked like—I can't help wondering if I could pass him on the street and not know, and yet I—I couldn't take being hurt like that again.'

He touched her hand softly, a wordless sympathy, then he reached for the picnic basket. She accepted a sandwich from him, and bit into it. 'Salmon? Do you think David caught this with his own hands?'

'With his net, more likely.'

They ate in a companionable silence. When the food was gone, Jenny leaned back and closed her eyes, the sound of the ocean a song in her ears. She drifted, listening, comfortably curled against a big log that had drifted in on a high tide.

Strange, she should have felt uncomfortably vulnerable after confiding in Jake. She'd shared a secret part of herself with him, given him a weapon. Yet his eyes told her that he would never use it against her. And she believed him.

He was leaning back against a log. He didn't look like a restless city artist. She smiled and his brows lifted in query.

'You look like a beach bum,' she said, laughing. He reached a hand across to her and she came, protesting weakly, 'Jake——'

'Relax,' he insisted softly, settling her against his broad chest.

Relax. It was the last thing she should do, lying here with him at the edge of nowhere, his heat flowing into her through the thin shirt he wore. But she closed her eyes again, settling comfortably against him, enjoying the feel of her cheek pressed into the curve of his shoulder, his arm holding her close.

An hour stolen from fate, a fantasy hour. She looked, and found his eyes closed, the lines of his face smoothed with contentment. She studied him freely...the off-centre fold in his right eyelid, the pale white scar that drifted up into his hairline.

Lance's face was a dim memory, but Jake's would be engraved on her mind for ever. She watched his nostrils widening as he took a deep breath, felt his chest rise beneath her face. Was he sleeping?

She let her fingers spread across his chest, startled as his free hand came up to cover hers.

How had he come by the scar on his forehead? A childhood accident?

His lids opened, the black lashes sweeping up. The fold she was watching disappeared and his brows rose in a question.

'Did I sleep?' He yawned, then laughed. 'I guess I did. Have you been trapped here for long?' His arm tightened around her momentarily, then relaxed. 'I thought I just closed my eyes for a second.'

'At least an hour.' She added whimsically, 'I was watching you.'

'And what did you see?' He was smiling, but she saw a trace of unease in his dark eyes.

She touched his forehead fleetingly. 'How did you get that scar?'

'Being a young fool. Were you speculating on the origins of my battle scars?'

'You looked content,' she mused. 'As if there were no place else in the world you'd rather be. You should come here more often, Jake. It's good for you.'

'Maybe it's you that's good for me,' he said suggestively.

She sat up abruptly, all the old uncertainties and fears washing over her. She brushed at sand, shaking out her shoes, avoiding his eyes. 'Don't—I doubt it. I've been around for years.'

'That was Jennifer,' he said softly. 'This is Jenny. Mind you, I still see glimpses of the elusive Jennifer, but sometimes I think George dropped her overboard with your hair.'

'Stop making fun of me,' she said uncomfortably. She stood up and started organising the picnic basket, looking around for any mess they might have left from their lunch. She badly needed to get this conversation back to normal, to put some barrier between them. 'I've been working on a film on this trip—on wildlife. You'd be amazed at what we've seen coming down from Alaska. Dolphins, a big whale, sea lions.'

He said, slowly, as if he wanted to bring back the intimacy of a moment ago, 'I got that scar when I was seventeen, having a damn fool argument with my cousin.' He laughed, embarrassed at his memories. 'He was bigger than me, but that didn't stop me trying to light into him.'

'What happened?'

Jake shrugged. 'I tried to hit him. He succeeded in hitting me. I ended up smashing into the stabilisers on the boat, cut my face wide open. Then we both went into the water. That cooled us off, and when my uncle got back he went after both of us.' He shrugged, grinning sheepishly. 'I can't even remember what we were fighting over. I told you, I got the scar being a damned fool kid— I'd like to see that film you're doing.'

She said defensively, 'It won't be an award winner, but I might manage to sell it.'

She found herself letting Jake draw her out on details, despite her suspicions about why he was interested. '...right now, my most pressing need is for a second video-recorder. I'm getting so many bits and pieces of tape, I need to get it edited.'

They were back at the truck. She stepped up into the cab, and Jake closed her door, then walked around the front to the driver's side.

His long legs showed lean and hard through his tight jeans, revealing muscles that his city clothes concealed.

Was the rest of his body as darkly brown as the part she could see? She glanced down at her own hand, remembering his dark skin against her pale fairness, shuddering with a raw wave of desire that left her weak and frightened.

He pulled the driver's door open and jumped up into the seat beside her. She sat tensely beside him, uncomfortably aware of how badly she wanted to be held in his arms again.

The engine roared to life as he said, 'I'll bring a recorder up to Queen Charlotte next week. And, Jenny—don't belittle your talents. You're good.' He turned towards her and gave her the full force of his smile, saying gently, 'But neither one of us is half as good alone as we are together.'

She took a deep breath, and stared ahead through the window of the pick-up. 'It had to come down to that, didn't it, Jake? You want me back at work. I'm not coming.' She gave an angry toss of her head, but there was no long hair to send sweeping back. 'This film is not something I'm doing for you. There's no need for you to supply my equipment.'

He changed the subject, startling her with a swift, 'What have you got against Hans?'

She managed to shoot back, 'I didn't say anything against him.'

'Yes, you did. This morning. Back at the boat—well, you snorted. Very expressively. I'd like to know why.'

'It's nothing.'

'Stop hiding, Jennifer! Come out with it!' The truck lurched into motion as Jake let out the clutch with an uncharacteristic jerk. 'We've had enough playing around, pretending things are fine when they're not. Don't you think it's time for some honesty?'

Angry, she pulled her seat-belt across and snapped it. She said tightly, 'Anything I said about Hans would sound like sour grapes.'

'Why?' He shot a startled look at her, then snapped his eyes back to the road as they hit a rough pot-hole.

'Because—because he's doing all the things I wanted to do. He's taken over all the best parts of my job. Why is that, Jake? Why did you put Hans in my place?'

He shifted up, then down again as another monstrous pot-hole appeared in the road. 'I—I thought you didn't want the job any more,' he evaded. 'You quit. You left and—aside from—do you have anything specific against Hans?'

If she said anything against Hans, Jake might think it was only resentment of her own loss in position. She glanced at him, found his face intent, his eyes on the road as he negotiated the pot-holes. He threw her a quick glance, telling her that he wouldn't drop the subject. She bit her lip, wishing for a distraction.

Jake's voice was carefully neutral as he prodded, 'I'll admit he's sometimes disappointing, but he did that film for Manley—that was quite a job.'

Heaven knew why she'd covered for Hans so long! She'd resented his presence, worried that he would damage Austin Media, worked frantically at times to cover his errors and omissions.

Jenny looked at Jake's strong determination, then away—at the sky...the sea...the road ahead. He said he wanted honesty, but—— With a shock she realised that hiding things from Jake had become almost second nature to her. In trying to conceal her strong attraction to him, she'd begun to conceal everything—her opinions, her resentments, her knowledge of Hans' inadequacies.

Disconcerted by her own sudden uncomfortable self-knowledge, she said abruptly, 'He didn't do the Manley film. He did a few shots, then skipped off to be with some girl while you were out of town. I put the film together—I had to, or you would have missed the deadline.'

Jake frowned, demanded, 'It's not the only time you've covered for him, is it? No, of course it isn't. That explains a lot of things.' Jake inexplicably dropped the subject, saying, 'Jennifer, look out there! The fishing fleet is heading out. Not the trolling boats like David's, but the seiners—the net boats.'

The sun came blazing through the open windows of the pick-up. Jenny felt suddenly relaxed, easy, able to enjoy Jake's company. Until the moment when Jake parked the truck near the docks, shoved the emergency brake on, then said with grim determination, 'About Hans—would you come back if he were gone?'

Incredulously, she said, 'You'd get rid of him just to get me back to work?'

'If that's what it takes.' His hands still gripped the wheel tightly. He was looking out of the front window as if he were still driving.

Jenny pulled on the door-latch, found it stuck and pulled again, desperately. 'Well, don't fire Hans just for me. I'm not coming back, Jake.'

Jenny almost fell out of the truck as the door suddenly swung open under her struggles. David MacDougal appeared at the top of the ramp and Jake said, 'There's David. He's taking me to the airport.'

He leaned across the seat and gripped her wrist with a strong, brown hand. She felt a shuddering wave of weakness at his touch, kept her face turned away from him as he said, low-voiced and determined, 'You will come back to me, Jenny Winslow. Sooner or later, you're coming back.' She shook her head, glancing at him with traces of panic in her eyes, shivering at the determined conviction in his.

He bent suddenly closer, brushing his lips against hers with a shocking, electric caress. 'Take care,' he whispered. 'Promise? Don't do anything crazy?'

'Jake——' she breathed, her eyes tangling deeply with his. Her hand found the side of his face in an involuntary caress. 'I——' Was she crazy? A total fool? Remember Jake and Monica...Jake and so many other women. She jerked away and waved brightly to David who was fast approaching the truck.

Her voice showed none of her inner bitterness as she said, 'You'd better get back to Monica.'

He looked startled, opened his lips as if to protest. Jenny couldn't help wondering what he would have said if David hadn't reached the truck in that instant.

'All ready to go to the airport, Jake? We'd better move it, or we'll miss your plane.'

CHAPTER SEVEN

JENNY swung from her perusal of the mountains to stare at George. 'What did you say?'

George's voice was mild as she repeated, 'Settle down and think about something else for a while. Jake will get here when he gets here.'

'I wasn't thinking about Jake,' Jenny denied weakly, but her cousin wasn't fooled.

'Nonsense! Ever since you called to tell him that we've arrived in this unpronounceable bay, you've been jumping up, staring at the sky, looking for seaplanes. You're obviously not getting over him. I think it's time you made a play for him.'

Jenny sat down abruptly on a log. 'George, he's in love with Monica!'

'Did he ever say so?'

'He said——' Jenny hesitated, then finished, 'He said he'd probably marry her.'

'Probably?' scoffed George with an unladylike snort. 'If he's marrying her, why is he chasing all over the North Pacific after you?'

Jenny said, dully, 'He wants me to go back to work.'

George's brows went up. 'If he were my almost-fiancé, I wouldn't be very pleased when he hops on a plane to Alaska at a moment's notice—just to have a little chat with you, you say. Next he's burning up the wires, sending out search parties because you're a bit late into Masset—then flying up to meet you on arrival. Where is Monica while he's doing all this? Now he's back again, just to guide you through these famous narrows. Don't you think he could find someone else to show us the way, if he really wanted to be with his Monica? The man's related to half the fishermen on these islands. He could get a cousin or a friend to guide us. But, no! He's got to come and do it personally, bring his Jennifer to safety. And if that doesn't mean——'

'It doesn't mean anything!' Jenny spun around in the sand, glared at George for a crazy minute, then shrugged helplessly. 'It means he's missing my work. You don't realise how important Jake's work is to him—it's more important than anything else.'

'More important than Monica?'

'Definitely,' said Jenny with certainty, remembering Jake breaking a date with Monica for the sake of a chance to get just one more shot with that camera.

'But you're part of that work.' George was thinking aloud, remembering the fierce look in Jake's eyes as he'd met Jenny on the wharf at Masset. 'So just which is the most important—you or the job—now that he has to separate them in his mind?'

Jenny shook her head and George said swiftly, concern for her cousin evident in her voice, 'You can't let one bad experience mess up your whole life. I know something happened to you. I had no idea then, but thinking back, remembering—it was Lance, wasn't it?'

'Yes,' Jenny admitted, her mind going back to the days after George had married Scott.

As children, she and George had been constant companions. Jenny hadn't needed any other close friends. Even when George married, Jenny's growing relationship with Lance had insulated her from loneliness.

Until Lance left.

Her brief ecstasy of love had ended bitterly. Jenny had been left alone, isolated, living in Aunt Georgina's house, walking to and from school, always seeming to be on the outside, looking in on other people's lives. There had been no one to help her through her misery.

George was frowning as if she had somehow tuned into Jenny's memories. 'Honey, part of your agony was adolescence, and immaturity, but—loving does make you very vulnerable. But it's worth it, Jenny. It really is.'

George had started a fire and wrapped some clams in seaweed, then heaped hot coals over them. Now she was picking them apart with a stick and fingers that jerked back every time the hot clam shells burned again. Watching her, Jenny couldn't help smiling.

'George, no one would believe that last year you were eating *escargots* in a famous restaurant in France.'

'I'm versatile,' mumbled her cousin around a hot mouthful of clam that she had just dipped in butter. 'Now shut up and eat some of it!'

'Delicious!' Jenny agreed, but she had no appetite. She ate three, then said, 'I'm going for a walk. Come with me?'

'No. I'm feeling a bit woozy— I think my legs haven't adjusted to dry land. I keep feeling as if I'm still moving.'

Jenny hadn't walked more than a few steps when she heard the engine of the seaplane. She swung around, searching the sky in the direction where she thought Queen Charlotte must be. She couldn't see anything at all, then suddenly she saw the seaplane, large and close and dropping for a landing.

She caught herself waving wildly before she could make out Jake sitting beside the pilot. She pulled her hand down to stop, but then he waved back and she ran down the beach and launched the dinghy, getting her feet wet without even noticing.

She must have left one oar on the shore. She couldn't find it. She grabbed the other one and started to paddle out to the seaplane. The propeller was slowing to a stop, the seaplane just drifting in the bay a few yards away from the boat.

He grasped the side of the dinghy as she came up against the pontoon.

'Hi, Jake.' She was breathless, the blood rushing to her head and making it feel funny, tingly and odd. She licked her lips nervously.

'Hi, yourself.' His eyes probed hers deeply, making her dizzy with the intimate contact. He turned and called back to the seaplane pilot, 'Thanks, Luke!'

The pilot stepped out on to the far pontoon, looking around, smiling slightly. 'Peaceful here today, isn't it?' he said, grasping the strut overhead with a large, muscular hand. 'Sometimes the wind howls through that opening—I wonder if the fish are biting? I think I'll try a couple of casts before I go.'

Jake climbed into the dinghy, touching Jenny's shoulder in a brief, casual caress. 'How are you? How was your trip? Where's the other oar?'

'I left it on shore. I paddled out.'

'Sit down, then.' His eyes were intent, examining every detail of her appearance, travelling from her face, down to the trembling hands folded in her lap. 'Don't you know better than to come out on the water without a life-jacket on?'

Jenny glared at him, then back at the seaplane that was quickly getting smaller as Jake swept the dinghy towards shore.

'I was going to ask you to come ashore and share some of our clams,' she told him, but she thought her own voice seemed far away and unreal as she went on '—fresh baked and delicious—but if you're going to start yelling at me the minute you arrive, I'd appreciate it if you'd just turn around and get back on that seaplane. It's still there. I'm sure you could get a ride back.'

He was silent for a moment, facing away from her and pulling heavily with the paddle. Then he stopped, motionless as the little dinghy continued to shoot along the glassy water, slowly losing speed.

'I'm sorry if I shouted.' He turned and looked at her at last. His face was rather sombre, the lines deep. 'I do worry about you—you and George, taking on these waters without——'

'Without a man?' she finished, her voice wry.

'I suppose,' he agreed slowly, still watching her from worried eyes. 'Yes, I suppose that's what I mean. Though I still worried when I thought George was a man, but—will you promise me to wear your life-jacket?'

'I usually do.' Today she had been so excited, seeing that plane coming, knowing he was in it. 'I feel a little funny today,' she admitted slowly. 'I might be a bit unhinged from sailing out on the west coast.'

'Was it rough?' he sympathised with a bit of a smile.

'Not really. We had good winds, perfect for sailing. Except one day—I was disgustingly sick. I wouldn't have believed how much motion there was. I don't think I was really meant to be a sailor. Not just the wind and the water, but ...' She trailed off, losing track of her thought.

'What?' asked Jake sharply.

She rubbed her hand across her lips. Perhaps she'd got salt on them from the water. They were tingling oddly. 'Nothing. I just——' Her tongue stumbled and she lost track again. She reached up a hand to rub the tip of her ear. '—but there was always a swell, up and down, the wa-wave ...'

'What's wrong with your ear?' he demanded in a voice suddenly harsh.

'Don' shout.' She rubbed the ear again. 'Don' shout at me, Jake. I——'

'Did you say clams?'

She shook her head, trying to concentrate over the dizzy tingling, and said weakly, '...George baked them.'

'Is your ear tingling?' He was shouting again, demanding, 'The tip of your ear? And your tongue? Damn it, Jenny! Answer me! Is your tongue tingling?'

'Yesh—yes.' Her tongue wasn't working at all, as if she'd been drinking too much.

'How many clams, Jenny?' The boat was moving again and Jenny slid down in the seat to let her head relax. 'Jenny!'

She shook her head, wishing he would stop shouting.

'How many clams, Jennifer?'

'...two...three...George had lots.'

'Damn!'

Jenny closed her eyes, realising that it was all a dream. It had seemed too real, but now it was receding, Jake's voice echoing as if she were spinning away from him and he were shouting into the distance. 'Luke! Fire it up again! We've got to get them into the hospital! Red Tide!'

Red? That was funny. The water was blue...not actually blue, but more of a green. The tide came in and went out again, but it wasn't red. She felt so odd. As if her body were moving in and out with the tide. She touched her lips with her tongue—felt nothing and re-alised it was the dentist who had frozen her mouth. He'd turn up any minute and start drilling.

Jake drove the dinghy into shore with hard, desperate strokes of the paddle.

Jennifer! Her head was resting on the gunwale, her eyes closed. God, was she actually breathing? Her chest moved, or he thought it did. He shipped the paddle, leaned over her, desperately looking for a sign, feeling a sagging relief as he felt the warm movement of her breath against his face.

He wanted desperately to get Jennifer to the seaplane, get her to a doctor. But George was on shore, probably in worse condition than her cousin. He gave Jenny another worried glance, then dashed ashore to pick up an unconscious George.

Luckily, George was still breathing. He hadn't stopped to think how he could administer artificial respiration while paddling the dinghy. What if Jennifer stopped breathing while he was carrying George to the dinghy?

What if she never opened her eyes again, never challenged him with that cool reserve again?

Once he had lifted George aboard, he paddled the dinghy swiftly back to the seaplane, his heart thundering in his ears so that he wouldn't have heard Luke if he'd been shouting. Luke, the tough-looking seaplane pilot, had the back door open and waiting.

'I think she's just stopped breathing,' gasped Jake as he handed George to the pilot. 'She'll need mouth-to-mouth.' Luke bent over the blonde woman's still body.

Jake picked Jenny up, felt her warm body sagging in his arms. If only she would show some sign of life! He strapped her into the front seat. She mumbled something as he fastened her seat-belt. He couldn't hear what she said, but he was grateful for even that small sign of life.

'Take it easy, hon,' he whispered, not knowing if she could hear him or not. 'You'll be OK, just keep breathing while we get you to the hospital!'

She looked so helpless, so vulnerable. He felt terrified himself, looking down at her, knowing the danger of the insidious paralytic shellfish poison that was flowing in her veins.

They had to move fast, but it all seemed to take so long. Strapping in Jenny, arranging George so that Jake could take over breathing for her. And Jenny—what if she quit breathing, too?

Luke closed up the doors, did a record-quick pre-flight inspection that seemed to take for ever, then got the Beaver into the air—fast, if not smoothly. Jake heard him calling in an emergency request to his base station.

'Get an ambulance down to the seaplane base! I'm bringing in two victims of Red Tide. Both of them unconscious.'

'Jennifer?' asked Jake, breathlessly, without breaking the rhythm of breathing into George's lungs. His own lungs were bursting, his mind desperately listening for

Jennifer as he maintained the rhythm of George's breathing.

'She's OK,' Luke called back. 'Still breathing.'

She couldn't die. She mustn't!

The summer Jake was fourteen, two tourists had been flown out of Cumshewa Inlet after taking a large feed of clams. The helicopter had flown in only minutes after a third member of the party called for help on the radio.

One of the men had died before he reached hospital. The other had been hospitalised in critical condition.

How many clams had they eaten? He couldn't remember. Jennifer said she had eaten only three, but she'd been confused, fuddled by the poison in her blood. God, Jenny! She couldn't die. He couldn't let her. If she died——

He blew a measured breath into George's lungs, his mind filled with a vision of a world without Jennifer. 'Jennifer?' he gasped between breaths.

Luke's voice came back, confident and reassuring, 'She's still OK—we're coming down for our landing now. I can see the ambulance waiting for us.'

In the moments of landing, Jake suffered an agony of apprehension as the seaplane bumped over the waves, taxiing in to the wharf. An ambulance attendant stepped up as the pilot opened the back door, taking over the rhythm of breathing for George as the pilot lifted her down to the stretcher.

Jake, finally free of his obligation to breathe for George, scrambled through the space between the seats, freeing Jenny from the seat-belt, lifting her into his arms and finally feeling the miracle of her warm breath on his cheek.

From outside, a second attendant opened the front passenger door. Jake shook his head, saying, 'I've got her. She's breathing. You look after the other one.' He couldn't let her go, couldn't give her up to anyone else's arms.

He carried her to the ambulance, his eyes watchful for any sign of change in her breathing.

How long since she'd eaten the clams? It must be almost an hour. The worst symptoms usually appeared within half an hour. Was that right? Or was it some piece of false folklore he'd picked up?

One attendant was working over George. The other bent over Jenny, lifting her wrist to take a pulse reading.

'She's breathing,' Jake said. 'How is her pulse? Is it all right? Do you think——'

'Clams? Or mussels?' asked the attendant.

'Clams. Do you think she's all right?'

The attendant shrugged. 'She's still breathing.'

She rested across his lap in the seat of the ambulance as they tore across to the hospital. Once she opened her eyes and stared at him without sight. Surely any movement was a good sign? He tightened his arms on her. 'You're OK,' he said firmly, hoping he was telling the truth. 'Just relax.'

She had to live. He wasn't sure what she wanted, why she had been so insistent on leaving him, but he knew now that he needed her to make his life complete.

He'd known it, subconsciously, ever since the first day she walked into his studio. She'd walked into his life and the sun had started shining brighter. Life had become exciting, a new challenge.

Not just his working life. Jennifer had spoiled him for any other woman. She had never given herself to him in passion, but he'd found himself comparing every other woman to her. He couldn't kiss a woman without wishing she was Jennifer. He'd tried to fight it, tried to tell himself it was only a desire for what he couldn't have.

It was much more than that. She was the one woman in the world who belonged at his side. For ever.

She had to get better. The thought of a life without her—he swallowed a lump that he knew was tears. He wanted her alive, alert, even fighting him if she had to.

As long as she was alive, there was a chance that somehow they might be together.

Could the poison still reach her diaphragm, paralysing it and causing her breath to stop?

At the hospital, she was taken from him. He had to force himself to let her go, knowing she needed the care of doctors and nurses, yet desperately afraid that he would never see her again.

A woman in a white uniform pushed his long form into a chair, seated herself behind a typewriter and demanded, 'Name?'

Barely concentrating, he answered automatically, 'Jake Austin.'

'Not your name! The patient's—first, the blonde woman. The one who isn't breathing.'

Dear God, that sounded terribly ominous! What if Jennifer—— He forced himself to concentrate, then said, 'George—Georgina Dobson.' But her name was almost all he knew. He couldn't answer any of the other questions asked by the records clerk.

'We have to know about medical insurance—how long has she resided in BC?'

'I've no idea,' Jake said helplessly. 'You'll have to wait for that.'

'If she's not a resident, she'll have to——' The woman hesitated, continued, 'Someone will have to pay for her hospital stay. She's not covered by hospital insurance unless——'

'I'll pay,' he said impatiently. 'Could you please find out how they're doing? What was the doctor's name?'

The woman pulled the multi-copy form out of the typewriter and presented it for his signature, then wheeled a second form into the typewriter.

Jennifer. My God! What if she stopped breathing while this woman was asking him foolish questions? He should be with her, he had to be where he could see her, know she was still breathing, that she hadn't left him for ever.

'Her birth date?' repeated the woman impatiently.

He didn't even know when Jennifer's birthday was! How could she work for him for five years, as closely and intimately as they had worked together, and he not even know her birthday? She must have come to work on her birthdays, and he had driven her—as always—to give everything to his films, and he hadn't even said 'Happy Birthday'.

Eventually, he was released from the small office and permitted to pace back and forth across a waiting-room until a tiny, dark-haired nurse came and asked,

'Hi, Jake. Can I get you a cup of coffee?'

He stared at the Haida nurse and she said, 'I'm Donna. Remember me, Jake?'

'Donna—of course. I'm sorry. I didn't recognise you. Do you know how they are? Is Jennifer all right?'

'Mrs Dobson is pretty bad. She's in intensive care—I shouldn't be telling you that, but the doctor is with her, working over her. The other one——'

He asked, 'Jennifer?' and stood very still, hardly breathing until she answered,

'She'll be all right. The doctor looked at her and he says she couldn't have got very much. Was it clams or mussels?'

'Clams. She said she had three.'

'Lucky for her. That's the first anyone's heard of Red Tide over there. Last year there was a bad bunch taken on Langara Island—luckily, no one died of it.' She glanced at a paper in her hand, and said, 'The fisheries officer called. He wants to talk to you—I've got the number for you to phone.'

'You're sure Jennifer's all right?' He glanced down at the slip of paper she handed him. 'Word gets around fast, doesn't it? All right. I'll call him later. Right now, could I see——'

She shook her head regretfully. 'Jake, they won't let anyone in to see Mrs Dobson. She's in intensive care. Until she's stabilised——'

'Can I see Jennifer?'

'Well——' She looked over her shoulder, then said warily, 'The doctor might prefer her not to be disturbed.'

'Please, Donna?' He had to see for himself, know she was all right. He found himself pleading, promising, 'I'll stay out of the way.'

'Oh, all right.' Donna grimaced. 'You'll drive us all nuts if you keep prowling around the waiting-room. Come on, I'll take you.'

For perhaps the first time in his adult life, he was conscious of trying to walk softly, quietly, into the room where Jennifer was sleeping, her face terribly pale, the blankets tucked tightly over her still form.

'Are you sure she's all right?' he whispered as Donna swept the curtain aside and let Jake in beside her bed.

'She's breathing, isn't she? Nothing will happen now—if it's going to get her, it does it quickly. She just has to sleep it off. Now sit quietly here, Jake, and don't cause me any trouble.'

'I won't,' he promised.

'Better not,' she threatened, grinning swiftly at him. 'I remember what a terror you were. You were always in trouble in the village.'

'I've reformed,' he insisted and she laughed as if she knew better.

Then, finally, he was alone with Jennifer.

On one side of the bed, a stand held a plastic sac of saline solution, a tube leading down to Jennifer's arm, connected to a needle in the back of her hand. He stared at it, seeing the needle going into her skin where it peeked out from the tape on her arm. He hated to think of her dependent on that fluid for her well-being. Was she really all right, or had Donna——

She had to be all right. He couldn't bear to think of any other possibility.

Jake moved the chair to the other side of the bed, drew it close. She would have a bruise there when the needle came out. He knew how easily she bruised. Once, she had stumbled on the stairs outside his studio. He had caught roughly at her arm with his hand, afraid she would tumble down the long stairs. For a second she'd been close to him. He'd breathed in the tantalising scent of her, his arm moving to draw her closer as she'd stepped away.

The next day, she had come to work wearing a blouse that concealed the purple bruise until she lifted her arm and the fabric fell away.

When he tried to apologise, she had shaken her head. The long hair had fallen across her face, concealing her eyes from him.

Now, the hair was short, curling softly around her head, leaving her face vulnerable and exposed. Her lips parted and she made some noise deep in her throat as her head moved restlessly on the white pillow.

When he covered her small white hand with his, her fingers curled loosely around his thumb. He stared at her pale fingers, wondering if she would ever put her hand in his willingly, freely. If only she would open her eyes, see him!

He sat quietly, watching her, sometimes staring through the window near her bed. He watched the cloudy sky turn from blue to red, remembering the words they had said to each other over the last five years, all the times when he'd almost come close to her.

Last week, on the beach near Tow Hill, she'd lain in his arms while he pretended to sleep. He'd felt her body so soft and trusting against his. He'd ached to draw her even closer, to cover her lips with his and draw a response from her. To love her, to touch and caress and take the loneliness away from her.

He'd been wrong to hire Hans. At the time, he'd thought it would help, putting a barrier between them.

He'd created a barrier all right, but it hadn't helped. Seeing less of Jennifer hadn't made him want her less. If he'd been honest with himself back then, faced the fact that he loved her, he might have been able to do something to win her.

When Donna returned, she found Jake still sitting, his hand entangled with Jennifer's.

'I brought you a coffee. I didn't know what you take—cream and sugar?'

'Thanks, Donna.' He remembered her now, a small girl from the village. She'd lived in the house below his grandfather's. He asked, 'How's Daniel?'

'He's still fishing. Fishing's not so good any more. A few years ago, the herring was big, but now it's down to almost nothing. We've got three sons now, you know.'

Jake nodded, though he hadn't known.

'Come and see us. We're in the village. Bring her, too.' Donna nodded towards Jenny. 'What's her name?'

'Jenny. She likes to be called Jenny.'

He sipped the coffee awkwardly, not wanting to let her hand go. He had to practise that in his mind. Jenny—not Jennifer. Why had she never told him before?

Visiting hours must have come. Outside the curtain, he heard voices, someone talking to the woman in the bed on the other side of the room. The doctor came, pushing a thin hand through his thinning hair, then taking Jenny's hand from Jake's grasp and staring at her face as he took her pulse, bending to lift her eyelid.

'Is she all right?' Jake asked nervously.

'She's lucky,' he growled. 'The other one—Mrs Dobson—is having a rough haul. I think she's going to make it.'

'Thank God,' murmured Jake. George seemed a nice woman and he wouldn't have wanted her to die of the poison, but he couldn't help being thankful that it hadn't been Jenny who had made a big feed of the clams.

'You may as well go home,' the doctor announced. 'She won't wake up for hours yet.'

'I'd rather stay.' Jake took possession of her hand again, looking up at the doctor with a determined glint in his eye. The doctor shrugged.

'Suit yourself,' he said as if he were too tired to oppose Jake.

He half expected someone to come and try to evict him at the end of visiting hours. No one did.

After a time, he dozed in the chair, waking with a sudden jolt of alarm, sitting up and staring intently at Jenny. He'd been dreaming, the fantasy tangled with reality. In his dream, Jennifer had stopped breathing, not responding to his futile, desperate attempts to revive her. In reality, she was breathing softly, her mouth slightly open.

He looked up and found his aunt standing at the end of the bed, her beautiful black hair glistening down her back, her sharp black eyes taking in everything. She was only ten years older than him, but he remembered how she had always been the one to know when he was misbehaving as a youngster.

'Hello, Violet.' He spoke softly. 'How did you know I was here?'

'Laurie phoned me.'

'Laurie Mather? The radio announcer?' He grinned ruefully. 'Am I a news item?'

Violet shook her head, smiling and sending the black hair flowing. 'She's married to the pilot that flew you today.'

'Luke?' He looked down at Jenny, tried to concentrate on the people his aunt was talking about. 'Luke Lucas? Didn't I hear a radio piece last year with his name on it?'

'Laurie did that—on a rescue operation she and Luke were involved in. Search for a downed seaplane. That's when she met Luke.'

Violet had the secret smile of someone who could tell a story, but wasn't going to. Jake frowned, trying to tie together threads of his knowledge of island people. 'I thought Laurie was engaged to Ken McDonald?'

'You've been too long away from home, Jake. For a local, you're out of touch with us.'

'Yes,' he admitted, his eyes going back to Jennifer.

Violet's eyes noted his hand tangled with Jenny's. She said, 'I saw a film you did last week—the tourism one.'

'The sights of Vancouver? Yes?'

He watched his aunt shake her head slowly, the glorious, glistening black hair rippling over her shoulders. 'It made me sad, Jake. There was no art in that piece. Not like before. You used to do films, drawings— whatever you did had meaning.'

He looked down at Jennifer, sleeping on the hospital bed. 'She said the same thing,' he murmured. 'She accused me of being too ambitious, too commercial.'

'You're Haida,' his aunt said with a stern, soft voice. 'Haida have always been artists.'

He said, 'I'm only half-Haida,' and Violet laughed.

'I'm sure none of us are pure blood any more, Jake, but don't ever forget that the Haida is the best half.'

Her dark eyes travelled from his face, down to where his brown hand enfolded Jennifer's white one on the blanket. She was smiling now.

'She's your woman, Jake? It's about time.'

About time. His hand tightened on Jennifer's. She was breathing a little more rapidly now. In a few hours he thought she would probably wake. Then he had to start trying to make her see that they belonged together. Violet was right. It was about time, for both of them.

His love was afraid of loving, afraid of being hurt. He'd have to teach her, somehow, that she could trust herself to him.

The women couldn't have helped. He'd been dating one woman after another in an attempt to get his mind off Jennifer. No, that wasn't all. He'd kept hoping to see some sign of jealousy.

Stupid, especially considering her distrust of love and men. Telling her that he intended to marry Monica couldn't have helped, either. She must be thoroughly convinced that he was a philanderer, intending to marry Monica, yet chasing after Jennifer—for surely she must realise by now that he wanted more than to get her back to work?

He looked down at Jennifer's sleeping form. It had been close. A few more clams, and if he'd arrived a few minutes later ...

His world without Jennifer.

'It's not so simple as that,' he said wryly, answering his aunt at last. She laughed softly.

'It never is, Jake.'

The sleeping girl shifted. He felt her hand tighten in his. Soon she would awaken and pull her hand away.

Had it mattered to her, when he said he was going to marry Monica? 'Yes, I probably will,' he'd told her, succumbing to a sudden need to know if she would care.

He knew her well enough now to know that if she did care, she would have retreated, stepped back, run away from anything she might feel for him.

And she *had* left, quickly and abruptly, leaving Jake bewildered and shocked at the extent to which he missed her.

He'd wanted her for a long time. Once he had thought it was her aloofness that kept him attracted, but now he knew it was more than that. Perhaps, subconsciously, he had always known.

There would be no other women now, only Jennifer. It would take time, but he could be patient when he had to be. If only he could find a way to keep her near, to give him the time he needed.

He settled down in the chair, shifting to grip her hand more firmly.

'You're not coming to the house for supper?' his aunt asked.

'No,' he said softly, knowing somehow that she would understand. 'I'll stay here. Thanks, Violet.'

He stayed, holding her hand, until the night nurse came on duty and insisted on his leaving.

Jenny drifted in and out of a fog, dreaming dizziness, hearing voices she couldn't focus her ears on.

She dreamed that she was held in Jake's arms, curling against him until the world receded and there was only his arms and, once, his lips brushing against her temple.

Shouting. She dreamed of shouts, the roar of an engine, and finally the wail of a siren. The dentist gave her another needle, but why in her hand? Then, once, she opened her eyes and focused on her own hand, held tightly in another—large, brown, with Jake's lean fingers. His baby finger was crooked from some ancient accident of which she had never learned the story. Were there scars on the rest of his body?

Her eyes followed up, along his arm, to his face which was strangely smooth in sleep. Jake, holding her hand, sleeping in a chair beside her. She smiled, recognising her own dream as wishful thinking.

When she finally woke, she realised she was in a hospital room, but alone. The sun was angling through the window, still the early morning summer sun of northern latitudes.

Jake was nowhere around. Of course she had dreamed his hand-holding attention to her. Hospitals didn't allow visitors in the middle of the night.

What had happened to George? Red Tide, Jake had shouted. That was the last clear memory she had—Jake questioning her about the clams as she lost track of her answers in the dizziness.

She slept again, waking to the shock of a thermometer being inserted under her tongue, the sight of a nurse bustling away before Jenny could ask any questions. Then she dropped off to sleep again, but woke as the thermometer was withdrawn from her mouth.

'My cousin—George—is she all right?'

'You'll have to ask the doctor when he comes in.'

But Jake came first, striding in and throwing the curtain back, bringing the smell of the outdoors with him.

'Are you all right?' he demanded.

'I'm fine, but what about George? Have you heard——'

'She's going to make it.' He pulled a chair close to her bed and sat down, his eyes searching her face intently. 'It was close. She stopped breathing—— *Damn* it, Jennifer! Surely you had the sense to know that you shouldn't just shovel in clams without——'

'I do know about Red Tide—that's what it was, wasn't it? But we didn't hear any warnings on the marine radio.'

He shifted impatiently. 'Read the fisheries regulations! This is the north! There aren't hundreds of fisheries offices up here to test the clams from every beach. The whole north coast is closed for taking of bivalves—every year! Always! You take clams and mussels at your own risk!'

'Stop yelling at me, Jake! Glenda and David gave us clam chowder!'

'You can be sure they had reason to know those clams weren't contaminated. You could have killed yourselves! George damned near did kill herself!'

'She is all right? She really is all right?'

'She's fine. I checked on her this morning. She's weak, and they don't want her to have visitors yet, but I have a sort of a cousin who's a nurse here, and she checked George's chart for me. She's breathing on her own, and the doctor says she's out of danger. The doctor, by the way, was up all night with George. He's gone home for a much needed couple of hours' sleep. Jennifer, so help me, if you ever——'

She caught his hand with hers, said softly, 'We were stupid—I admit it! Thank goodness you came when you did—I don't know what would have happened, because we didn't know—of course I know about Red Tide. Every so often, we hear about someone falling victim to it, not heeding the warnings when an area is found to be contaminated, but I never even thought of it.'

Jake covered her hand with both of his. 'I should have thought of it when we had that chowder. I should have warned you. Next time, if you're determined to eat clams, take precautions. If you're careful, you can be reasonably sure you're safe—all right! I'll drop it for now, but remind me to give you my lecture on testing clams.'

'I will, I promise. You are sure George is all right? Can I see her?'

'I doubt it.'

She knew she should pull her hand away, but she left it in his warm grip. 'And you?' she asked. 'Shouldn't you be getting back to work?'

He shook his head. 'Not until I know you're both well.'

Jenny frowned at him, and said repressively, 'Isn't it time you got back to Monica?'

He shifted, gripping her hand tightly. 'Jenny, I wanted to tell you——'

'Do you know what time we get to eat?' she asked nervously, covering his words with the first thing that came to mind. God, she couldn't stand it if he started talking about Monica, if his eyes grew warm with wanting another woman! 'I'm just starving.'

'I'll check,' he said abruptly, getting up and walking away. She watched him going, feeling a sick knowledge that she was getting herself into a mess, loving him more and more every day, setting herself up for a big dose of pain and loneliness.

It was time she stopped fooling herself. She had loved Jake for years—perhaps from that first day when she had walked into his studio, finding him buried in paper, trying to get a series of drawings ready, his hair wild from running his fingers through it.

She had to move, get herself busy, stop thinking about Jake. Her legs were weak and shaky, but nobody tried to stop her from walking around, getting her strength back and exploring, even visiting George to confirm that she really was all right.

When visiting hours started, Jake was there again, striding down the hallway, stopping abruptly when he saw her standing near a window, saying softly to her, 'You're looking much better.'

She managed a casual smile. 'George is better, too. Sleeping, but she's all right now. I love this little hospital. All the windows look out on the harbour.'

Jake didn't say anything, just stared at her, his brown eyes almost black.

The silence was making Jenny nervous. 'I've got to thank you again for getting us in here so quickly. If George hadn't got to a hospital ...'

'Forget it,' he said gruffly.

Jenny said nervously, 'About *Lady Harriet*—George is worried——'

'The boat's all right. One of the fishermen is checking on her. He's going to tie up alongside her tonight, so no one will disturb anything. Then, tomorrow, I'll fly out and bring her back through the narrows.'

'Oh, good!' She'd been trying to work out a way to get the boat back, but she should have known Jake would look after it.

Jake smiled a slow, mischievous smile. 'You did say you didn't want me trying to run your life?'

She couldn't help smiling back. '*Touché!* Just this once, if you would be so kind as to be your usual domineering self—I would appreciate it!'

'At your service!'

She decided impulsively, 'I'll come with you tomorrow. The doctor said I could check out in the morning. I've nowhere to go, except to the boat, so ...'

Her voice dropped off slowly. Together on the boat, they'd be alone. She opened her lips to change her mind, but he said quickly, 'It's probably a good idea. I'll need help. You'll know all the details, like where George keeps the ignition key.'

'And I'll pay for the seaplane charter,' she added, hoping to strike an impersonal note.

He shook his head. 'You're rolling in money, of course.'

'I've got a little saved.'

'Keep it,' he said firmly, adding, 'Although I should let you pay for the charter—then you'd be short of money sooner. I might get you back to work that way.'

CHAPTER EIGHT

THE Beaver's pilot smiled at Jenny as he stepped on to the pontoon. He opened the rear door with large, capable hands.

'You're looking a lot better than when I saw you last!'

She found herself smiling back at him. 'I'm feeling better. Thanks for getting us to help so quickly the other day!'

'It was a fast trip.' He glanced at Jake. Something passed silently between the two men and Luke added, 'This trip will be slow and easy. I hear your cousin's going to be all right.'

'Yes, she's fine,' Jenny agreed, startled.

Jake gave her a hand up into the seat behind the pilot, then swung himself into position beside her.

'You'll get used to it,' he murmured. 'It's a very small community out here. News travels like wildfire. And Luke has an inside track on news. He's married to Laurie—she works at the radio station.'

'The radio station?' she asked, surprised. 'Were we on the radio?'

Startled, Jake said, 'I hadn't thought of that.' He leaned forward to Luke and asked a swift question, leaning back with a smile.

'Not yet,' he told her. 'But Laurie was going to go over to the hospital with her microphone this morning.'

'Good,' said Jenny. 'George is better at interviews. She can speak for both of us.'

'How are you liking my islands?' Jake asked her as he twisted to find the missing end of his seat-belt.

'I think I'm falling in love,' she said softly, without thinking how he might take her words.

'What?' Jake's voice was loud as his seat-belt snapped closed.

'Falling in love with the islands, I mean,' she added quickly, flushing and looking away from dark eyes that seemed suddenly filled with fire. 'There's a feeling out here; no one's in a hurry, but they all seem to care about each other.'

'They were in a hurry the other day, getting you two into the hospital. Do up your seat-belt, Jenn—Jenny.'

She fumbled with the mechanism. He took it from her. 'I'll do it—it's simple, really—like this. Watch as we go. I asked Luke to fly along the narrows so you can see it.'

'Wouldn't you have preferred to be in the front with the pilot?'

'I didn't think you'd care to be left back here by yourself.'

'Oh.' She stared at him for a second, then away.

'I am trying, Jenny,' he said softly.

'Trying to—to do what?'

Her eyes were drawn back to his as he said slowly, 'To mend my ways, I guess. Show you more consideration. I suppose I'm mostly trying to make you see it would be different if you came back.'

'Jake, I don't——'

'Don't say no, Jennif—Jenny. Just don't say anything. Not right now. Later, we can—— There, look down on your side! See the way the water narrows? See the rocks? No, don't be nervous. Think of it. Luke's got pontoons on this plane. He can set it down anywhere on this water.'

He shifted to point, leaning across her. She felt his breath warm against her cheek. His other arm slipped behind her shoulder for balance. She felt a sudden, overwhelming urge to lean back into the curve of his shoulder.

'What are all the colours?' she asked, breathless. 'And what did you tell the pilot? Did you say I was afraid of flying?'

His arm was still at her back. She should move away, just enough so that his shoulder stopped touching hers. She looked up, seeing the lines that spread out from the corners of his eyes. For a long silent moment their eyes were locked together. Unconsciously, her lips parted.

The corner of his lip moved in a slight smile as he shook his head. 'I said you weren't used to small planes, that's all.'

'I thought—the way he looked at you when he said it would be a slow and easy trip.'

'I didn't give away your big secret. Luke's probably pretty sensitive to people who are afraid. His wife was in a bad crash when she was——' He stopped abruptly, said swiftly, 'Sorry, Jenny. That's pretty stupid of me, bringing up that sort of thing when we're in the air. Those colours you asked about—look down here——' His hand cupped her shoulder, turning her to look out of the window again. 'That's the channel we'll be going through!'

'There's no room for errors, is there?' She was carefully still, feeling his hand on her shoulder, his arm along her back. She tried to keep herself from trembling. 'I'm glad George and I didn't try to go through alone.' She stared down through the window, unable to turn back without being far too close to Jake.

Abruptly, he moved back and she was alone in her seat, some contrary part of her wishing him closer again.

The seaplane banked, turning into a wider channel. Jenny looked down and saw *Lady Harriet* waiting below.

'What time do we go through the channel?' she asked as she looked down. George's boat looked very small from up here.

'First thing in the morning. We'll have to wake up early for it.'

So they would stay together on the boat tonight, alone. She glanced over at Jake, but he was studying the scene below as they circled for a landing.

Where would Jake sleep?

Don't be silly! It wouldn't be the first time she'd spent a night alone with him. Three years ago they'd gone up to an abandoned mill town to do a camera study that was later shown on national television. They had stayed in an empty house that had once been the mill manager's residence. Jake had slept on the sofa and Jenny in the master bedroom.

Nothing had happened. Of course nothing had happened. She'd been very aware of him in the next room, but finally she had slept.

At night, on the boat, she could usually hear George's breathing if she listened carefully. Tonight, she would listen for Jake's breathing.

'There's the dinghy!' Jake shouted in her ear. 'It's tied to the boat. Norman must have found it.'

'Was it lost?'

Jake's face seemed oddly pale as he answered, 'George stopped breathing just as I got you two to the plane. We piled in and Luke took off—we had to leave the dinghy drifting. At the time, it didn't matter—not nearly as much as getting to a doctor. But I'm glad it's been found. I'd have felt badly about that.'

'There's nothing for you to feel badly about. You saved our lives.' She stared down at the water rushing towards them, remembering the sudden dizziness that had overtaken her as she greeted Jake. She'd attributed it to seeing Jake again. 'Who's Norman?'

'A fisherman.'

'Another relative of yours? This place is loaded with your relatives.'

'I know.' He grimaced. 'It makes me feel a bit intimidated, especially when my Aunt Violet starts lecturing me. I have to look in the mirror to be sure I'm not suddenly fourteen again—no, Norman isn't one of the relatives. I went down to the docks yesterday to see who I could find to check out *Lady Harriet*. I'd never met Norman before, but he was just leaving to go out on the afternoon tide, so he volunteered.'

She frowned. 'Does anyone ever say no to you?'

'Yes.' He laughed. 'Recently, a little girl named Jennifer Winslow has been saying no quite consistently.'

She was five foot four, but from his height she supposed that would seem very small.

'Small only in size,' he amended. 'Here we are—it's going to be a perfect landing!'

It must have been. Jenny didn't feel the pontoons touching the water.

'It's calm,' the pilot called back. 'There's no reason I can't take you right over to the boat.'

She watched Jake and Luke working together, bringing the plane in nose first. Luke stood on the pontoons and held the Beaver against the side of *Lady Harriet*. Jake stepped aboard and reached down a hand for Jenny.

They stood on the deck together, watching the seaplane taxi away. As if they belonged together, alone on this vessel. Jenny quickly suppressed the thought.

The echoes of the engine slowly faded, leaving a silence that filled slowly...a sea bird crying from somewhere to their left...a faint, far-away echo of surf riding on the sand.

Jake pushed his hands deep into his pockets, something he often did just before delivering some deeply thought decision. But this time he only stared out at the water, then turned and said, 'Let's check the boat out. If there's anything wrong, we should find out as soon as we can.'

Everything was just as they had left it. Even the coffee-pot was still on the stove.

'Oh, lord! The coffee! We left it on the stove!' Jenny smelled it as soon as Jake opened the sliding hatch. She followed him down below, going immediately to where the coffee-pot sat on the cast-iron top of the enclosed oil cooking stove. 'That's our coffee from—when? Two days ago? That pot will be a mess!'

'Put some water in it and let it soak,' suggested Jake.

Jenny picked up the pot and turned on the water pump at the galley sink. She already had a scouring pad out, scrubbing at the black insides of the coffee-pot.

'It has to be cleaned sooner or later,' she muttered, 'but this isn't working.'

'Fill it with water and dump some sort of cleanser into it. We'll open up all the portholes and abandon ship while the fresh air takes over.'

Jake was prowling the insides of *Lady Harriet* restlessly.

'We'll go ashore,' he said again.

'You were going to tell me how to test clams for poison, weren't you?'

'Yes, well——' She thought he seemed oddly ill at ease. What was wrong? Had she said something, or was he wishing he were somewhere else—with Monica? 'Clams,' he said, staring at his feet, then looking up. 'It's not a perfect system—it involves somebody being a guinea pig, but only in a limited way. That person cooks and eats one clam, then waits for an hour to see if there's any tingling of the tongue or ears. If it's OK, the person should test again, eating two clams. If there are any symptoms, he takes a healthy dose of antacid—the organism reproduces in an acid environment—otherwise, if there are no symptoms, you can be pretty sure the clams are OK.'

Ashore, he took a stick and dug until he had located a butter clam. He cut it open with a pocket-knife, showing her the siphon which was known to be the location where the poison concentrated.

'If one clam on this beach is contaminated, they all are. The organism appears in the water in great concentration—that's the Red Tide. The clams siphon it out, along with their other food—and the whole area is contaminated. It takes a long time for it to get back to normal.'

Jenny shuddered, unable to imagine herself digging— or eating—clams again.

George's campfire was washed away. They walked along the sand, veering off through the trees. Jenny found the stunted trees fascinating.

'Even the bush is different here,' she marvelled. 'Anywhere else on the coast, the trees would be tangled with underbrush. Here you can walk through, just as if it had been cleared.'

'It's like that all over the islands. Just a green carpet of moss under the trees.'

'It's beautiful.'

She found a tree that must have been made for her to sit against. She sank down in the soft moss, curled against the trunk. She could see through the forest to the water and the beach.

Jake stopped walking, but didn't sit. He pushed his hands into his pockets again.

'Jenny, I've been thinking about what I've been doing—at work. I've thought a lot about what you said.'

'What did I say?'

'That I'm sacrificing quality in work, taking on contracts like the Madison training series.'

She shifted uncomfortably, admitting, 'I was angry, not thinking what was coming out of my mouth.'

He nodded. 'So you said things you'd never have said otherwise. That doesn't mean there wasn't some truth in what you said. I've been ambitious. Trying to prove something, I guess.'

He sounded almost defensive, unlike the Jake she was accustomed to seeing. 'What do you have to prove to anyone, Jake?'

He picked up a stick and absently started sketching a raven design in the sand. 'I got a lot of opposition from my father's people about going to art school. It wasn't practical, and they despised the Haida part of me. Haida have always been artists, and that was enough to set them against my ambitions to make a career of art. They hadn't wanted my father to marry my mother, and once she died they tried to pretend it hadn't happened.

'They couldn't stop me from spending my summers up here, and it was the summers that put me in tune with the artist in me—the tremendous heritage of Haida carving and art. My grandfather carved totem poles, you know.'

His grandfather, the Haida chief. 'Yes, I knew that.'

'He was a wonderful man—full of a slow-spoken wisdom that was terribly impressive to me. He helped me—not directly, because he wouldn't have told me to go against the wishes of my father's family—but he gave me the perspective to realise what I should do.

'They kept the pressure up all the time I was in art school—actually, I managed to avoid seeing my uncle. He lived in Victoria—still does—and he was the worst of them. I like the old beggar, but he led me a hell of a time back then. But once I started making a go of it, everything changed.'

She felt angry on his behalf. 'They accepted your art as a good thing then? After you proved yourself?'

His smile had a tinge of bitterness. 'At first I resented that, then I guess I got carried away with the success game. Deals like Madison came along and—well, the money was good, and the work——'

'You could put most of the boring work off on me,' she suggested softly.

'Yes, I was guilty there. You shouldn't have let me get away with that.'

She was watching the raven grow beneath his stick, the design turning into a two-dimensional totem pole in the sand. 'You don't need those jobs, Jake. You're doing well, making a name for yourself. You had that exhibition at the museum. Those modernistic totem pole prints from your drawings have been selling really well, and the couple of serious films you've done this last year have had a really good reception.'

He put a vicious beak on the raven with a swift stroke. 'I know that. I've had my head in the sand, not seeing what was going on. I thought about Hans, too. Took a real good look at him when I was back in Vancouver this last week. You were right about that, too. And Charlotte—she's really working out quite well. I haven't been around much, and she's been showing quite a talent for dealing with impatient clients. We could go back, Jenny. Send Hans on his way, go back to the way it was— you and I running the film-making—Charlotte could take over some of your work, the parts you don't like. We could train her—if you'd come back——'

She looked away, seeing the outline of the islands in the harbour as she thought about being back in Vancouver with Jake. It was hard to believe that he loved Monica, that he could leave her so easily if he really meant to marry her.

If she went back ...

The islands in the harbour faded, and Jenny knew that she was lost if she let Jake take her back to Vancouver. Her barriers against him were crumbling, and she'd find herself helpless and miserable, watching him with other women, perhaps even reduced to begging him for some crumb of love for herself.

'Jenny?' His hand was still, the totem in the sand unfinished.

She whispered, 'I can't, Jake. I can't go back.'

'Why not?'

He stood up, dropping the stick, his legs slightly astride to balance better. He looked like a man who never gave up, standing in front of her with the ocean behind him, his hands deep in his pockets, his face hard and deeply lined. He was dark, like the sea when it was angry.

'Not now, Jake,' she begged desperately, trying to gather her cool mask back around herself. 'Let's not talk about it now.'

She pushed herself up, slipped on the moss and found herself clinging to his hand as he supported her, helping her to her feet.

She came to her feet breathless, pulled up against his chest, pressing into the padding of his denim jacket. She stared up into his eyes. Then she was free of his arms, stumbling a little and starting to walk through the trees.

'Shall we have dinner on the beach?' she asked, not looking back at him. 'Not clams,' she added, thinking the subject of shellfish might distract him. 'There are potatoes on the boat. We could roast them or we could cut up stewing meat and potatoes and carrots and—you can do them all up together in tin foil and put them in the fire—it's delicious!'

'You must have been a boy scout.' She had the oddest feeling that he hardly knew what he was saying.

'Girl guide,' she corrected. 'I do know my way around a campfire.'

Back at the boat, Jenny opened the refrigerator in the galley and found it filled with a large, fresh salmon.

'There's a dead fish in the fridge,' she told Jake, giggling slightly.

'That must have been Norman.' Jake leaned over her shoulder to see. 'He was trying to give me a salmon when I was talking to him on the wharf, but I told him I had nowhere to put it.'

Jenny cut up carrots, potatoes and onions, then added butter, salt and pepper and wrapped the vegetables in

tin-foil bundles to put in the fire they would light on
shore. Jake prepared the salmon for baking and wrapped
it in foil, then rummaged in George's stores and found
a bottle of wine and some plastic glasses.

'We don't need plates,' he told her. 'Just forks—these
plastic ones I found will do—and we can eat right out
of the packages. Then we can burn the plastic and come
back without any dishes to do.'

'Jake, you're lazy!' she accused him, laughing. 'Afraid
to do a few dishes!'

He grinned and retorted, 'You've become so assertive
these days, I'd probably be the one washing the dishes.
And I really do hate dishes. I think we should——' He
stopped abruptly and she could have sworn he flushed
under his tan before he said weakly, 'Let's go ashore
now. We've got everything we need.'

On shore, he built a fire from driftwood they col-
lected, then they placed the packets of food carefully
where they would get heat, but not enough to burn. They
sat on rocks near the fire, quietly, comfortably, watching
the flames and sipping on their glasses of wine. Watching
Jake, Jenny wondered at the deep lines of his face, his
pallor that showed her he was going short of sleep.

When the food was done, they ate from the foil
packets, licking their fingers clean afterwards because
they had forgotten to bring napkins ashore.

'Come for a walk,' he urged as they watched the last
of their dishes turning to coals in the fire.

'A slow walk—I'm stuffed! That salmon was so good!
George and I must try to catch some salmon. Just
imagine! Reeling in a salmon, then cleaning it and
popping it straight into the oven for dinner!'

'Jenn—Jenny, watch where you're walking! The
ground there isn't very stable. Something's been tun-
nelling here.'

She stepped back, lurching a little as the ground under
her feet moved. Not surprising, she thought with a wry

smile. Around Jake, even the earth moves. His hand fastened on her arm and pulled her against him.

'Ouch! You're hurting my arm, Jake!'

'Sorry.' But he didn't let go. His arm slipped around her shoulders as he looked down into her eyes. 'It's not the first time I've done that, grabbing too hard.'

'You're rough,' she agreed, but his hand smoothing her hair was very soft and gentle.

'Jenny,' his voice was low and gruff on the salt air, 'I keep looking at you, expecting to see Jenny with the long, brown hair—like the song—I dream of Jenny.'

'The girl in the song had light brown hair.' Her voice was husky. She tried to make it firm and casual as she added, 'My hair isn't light. And she was Jeannie, not Jenny. And you don't dream of me.'

'So I rewrote the song.' He should have been smiling, but he wasn't. His hand was still lingering over her hair, his fingers caressing down, along the side of her neck.

Staring at him, her lips parted and her breath became ragged. If he would smile, she would know it was a joke. But he didn't. She managed an unconvincing laugh as she said shakily, 'That's Jake. If you don't like it, change it.'

He smiled then and her breath came back as he complained, 'You've gotten so damned argumentative, Jenny. You were never so blunt before.'

'I know—I'm surprising myself,' she admitted slowly. 'I guess I've run out of yeses.'

His hand stroked back up, his fingers combing through her short hair. His face was very close to hers; any minute now, he would kiss her. She could feel his intent and knew she should move away. He said softly, 'I like it, actually. I enjoy a good argument.'

'Not as much as you like winning,' she shot back at him.

'I don't——' He broke off, laughing ruefully. His hand dropped from her hair and she did move away, resisting the need to stay close. 'I suppose that's true enough, but—— Damn it, Jenny, what the hell are you doing! I'm chasing all over the damned countryside, Alaska, the Queen Charlottes—next it'll be Baha, Mexico. When are you going to come back?'

Her face froze and she said flatly, 'I'm not coming back, Jake. Not ever.'

She saw the lines around his mouth deepen as he said harshly, 'You've got to, Jenny. I need you.'

He needed her in his library, his studio. Not in his personal life. If it weren't for Monica, they might have an affair, now that she had realised how badly she wanted him. If she went back, though, it could only be a disaster. He might marry Monica—or, if he didn't, then eventually he would become Jenny's lover—because he wanted her, and one day she would be weak enough to open her arms to him.

She squeezed her eyes tightly closed, forcing herself to remember the lonely days after Lance.

She whispered, 'I don't belong to you, Jake.'

'Jennifer ...'

She stopped walking, turned to look at him. She managed to make her face a rigid mask that hid how badly she wanted him to move to her, touch her again.

He stared at her across the few feet that separated them. The sounds of the surf came distantly from the other side of the headland that formed the bay. Overhead, a bald eagle swooped in a slow circle, searching for prey.

Jake shoved his hands into his pockets, swinging away from her to pace restlessly along the sand, then prowl back. He stopped only inches away from her, hands still deep in his pockets, staring at her with dark, disturbed eyes.

She begged, 'Don't look at me like that, Jake!'

But he only stared more fiercely, his mouth turned down as he said, 'Jenny, come back. I want you to start directing. You're good at it—I'll do the photography and the artwork. You'll——'

'No, Jake!'

His eyes seemed to turn cold, with anger or some other emotion. His voice was as hard as the granite rocks. 'I can't just let you walk away!'

She forced her words out. 'You've no choice, Jake. I can't stay.'

'Why not? It's—since you left, I—it's not the same any more. It—I guess it's just not fun any more. The whole thing, the films, the projects—it's all lost its appeal.'

His hand slipped out of his pocket, grasped her arm and drew her closer to him, until she was only a hair's breadth away.

'Come back, Jenny,' he pleaded softly, 'please ...'

A breeze rippled along the water, sneaking up and around them, making Jenny shiver. Jake reached down to her shoulders, pulled her jacket closed and slowly fastened the top button. His hands lingered around her shoulders as he stared down into her eyes for an endless moment.

'Jake ...' He was going to kiss her. The intent was in his eyes. Jenny knew she should stop him.

Her lips parted slightly, her tongue slipped out to wet the sudden dryness. Jake watched the motion, mesmerised, his own lips moving slowly closer.

She trembled, waiting for his touch.

His lips brushed against her mouth. She shuddered, the light touch sending weakness through her whole body. She couldn't pull her eyes away from the deep, molten darkness of his gaze. It seemed to pull her closer, until she was pressed against the breadth of his chest, her breasts crushed against his hardness.

The weakness overtook her as Jake's arms tightened, drawing her into his kiss. Her eyes closed. His lips moved against hers, his tongue touching, exploring.

Her arms slid up around his neck, fingers spreading through the crisp black curls. At her back, his hands slid under her jacket, under the fabric of her blouse, exploring the smoothness of her skin.

As his hands slid around to caress her midriff, she felt a wave of heat spreading through the centre of her womanhood, a roaring in her ears.

Jake. Hands gentle, yet hot on her body. Lips drawing a trail of desire from the corner of her mouth, along her jawline to her ear, where he murmured her name.

Her hands slid down, tracing the shape of his neck, the contours of his chest. The murmur in her ear became a groan, responding to her touch.

'Jenny,' he groaned, his hands unfastening the jacket, finding their way through the barrier of her blouse and moving heatedly over the pale skin of her shoulders, the swelling of her breasts.

Her head tipped back, almost as if her neck had no strength. His eyes were molten, burning into hers as he groaned, 'God! Jenny, I've needed you for so long!'

His hands caressed the firm breasts as they swelled in response to him. She groaned his name as his thumbs rubbed over her erect nipples. She was clinging to him, her knees weak, her hands restless against the fabric of his shirt.

Her lips sought the area under his chin, her tongue reaching out to touch the soft, vulnerable skin of his throat. Then her hands fumbled their way through the buttons of his shirt, found the dark hairs on his chest and twisted their way through, drawing a groan from deep in his throat.

His arms surrounded her, lowering her on to the sand. Relieved of the need to support herself, her legs stopped trembling. Her heart stopped. Everything stopped as he pushed her blouse back and stared down at her with eyes that had turned black with his passion.

She licked her lips, staring up at him. His own lips parted in response, then he bent down, his mouth covering hers, his tongue thrusting, demanding a response, then suddenly, abruptly withdrawing.

Bewildered at his sudden withdrawal, she stared up at him, to find a dark uncertainty in his eyes.

'Jennifer?' he whispered a question. His eyes closed briefly, opened again and caressed the exposed mounds of her breasts.

Then his lips moved over the sensitive peak of her breast, touching, kissing, drawing her nipple deep inside his mouth with a gentle passion that had her shuddering, groaning his name, clutching at his shoulders.

His hand was moving over her hip, stroking, as his mouth drove her wild. He pulled her close and she could feel his hard need of her, her own body trembling, then tensing in response.

Then his hand was moving, loosening the waistband of her jeans, caressing the soft, vulnerable skin of her abdomen. Her hands clenched in the crisp black hair on his head, needing his lips on hers, drowning in the hard thrust of his tongue, answering his passion with her own, spinning away on a tide of need and sensuality as his restless hands found every sensitive part of her aching female body. His lips left hers again and heated her body with passion until she was a mass of desire, groaning beneath his touch, twisting against him, caressing him with her own heated hands.

'Jenny?' He whispered her name as his hand caressed the centre of her womanhood. She shook her head, not wanting to talk, only wanting his touch on her, her body against his.

'Are you sure?' he asked, his lips back against hers, touching hers with a softness that made her eyes open again.

Sure. Was she sure? She stared at him, seeing in his eyes the awareness of her own need of him. She was lying in his arms, half-naked, needing him as she'd never needed any man. Certainly Lance had never driven her to this state of desperation.

She closed her eyes, feeling her own woman's need of him like a pain.

'No.' It was only a whisper, but his hands fell away and she was alone and shivering, sitting up and trying to fasten her clothes with trembling fingers.

'Jennifer——'

'No! Don't say anything. Please, don't say anything. Can we just pretend it didn't happen?' She stood up, managing to meet his eyes.

'You've got to be joking,' he said, his own eyes still dark with his desire as they met hers, pleading yet defiant.

CHAPTER NINE

JAKE forced himself to step back in the soft sand.

'Jenny?' he said, his voice husky. 'Why did you leave me?'

Her eyes were startled, suddenly frightened as they met his. He asked carefully, softly, 'Did it have anything to do with Monica? I said I was going to marry her and——'

'No!' She shook her head violently, jerking away from him and moving swiftly along the beach towards the dinghy. He kept pace, his heart pounding with this new discovery. He'd seen the truth in her eyes in the moment before she'd turned away.

'Jennifer—Jenny, I'm not going to marry Monica. I never really intended to. I just——'

She swung back to face him, her eyes suddenly angry. 'Monica thinks you are,' she accused him swiftly, silencing him. She glared at him for a long second, then started launching the dinghy.

He closed his eyes briefly, painfully. A moment ago Jenny had been in his arms, his for the taking if he'd kept his mouth shut. But he wanted more than a brief possession of her body, and she was nowhere near ready for more.

Love! He could remember smiling a little wryly at the sweeping, all-encompassing passion of the novels.

He'd felt like that about his work at times, when the passion took hold and nothing mattered but the perfect shot, the struggle to draw the perfect line to complete a design. Jenny had been part of that, but somehow he'd never seen it clearly, never seen her clearly.

He helped her launch the dinghy, found himself having to hold back little impulses to touch, brush her hand or her hair with his hands.

'There's a boat coming in,' he said hoarsely as he held the dinghy steady for her to board.

'Will he tie up to us?' She was careful not to look at him as she stepped in.

'Probably not—there's another mooring.'

She edged away from him. Was she afraid he would start to make love to her again? Only moments ago she'd shared his need, but now she'd had time to think, to withdraw, to run away to safety.

Move carefully, he warned himself. Casually, he asked, 'Can I look at your film this evening? I'd like to see what you've done.' He slid the dinghy into the water, waving to acknowledge a greeting from the captain of the fishing-boat.

Jenny was silent until they were aboard. Then, as she watched Jake hooking up wires to the portable recorder he had brought, she spoke suddenly.

'Jake, I called Marty about this film. He's interested in buying it.'

He plugged in the last wire, switched on the recorder and said evenly, 'Naturally, he'd be interested. He's been trying to hire you ever since we won the award. Where's your camera, Jenny? And the tapes?'

She walked into her cabin and pulled out the camera case, brought it back and thumped it down in front of him.

He said sharply, 'Careful! That's a delicate instrument!'

Her voice was tense, her face expressionless as she demanded, 'Don't you care if I sell it to Marty?'

'*Of course I care!*' Jake realised he was shouting, and forced his voice quiet. 'I'd like to throw something, start shouting—but what the hell am I supposed to do about it? I'm trying to be restrained——'

'Oh, Jake!' She couldn't help laughing. He was glowering at her, fury and frustration flowing from him in waves. 'What am I going to do with you? Restrained? You? You start swearing every time you get upset!'

'I am trying,' he said, somewhat grimly. 'Here, give me the first film. Do you have notes? Are you going to give me a rundown, or should I just look?'

'Just look.'

'Is there any coffee? I'd like a cup while I watch this.'

'The coffee-pot——'

'Sorry, I forgot. No, J—Jenny.' Damn! He had to remember not to call her Jennifer! 'Don't start cleaning it now. Throw it overboard. We'll get George a new one as a getting-out-of-hospital present.'

She watched him as the film started. She saw when he stopped being aware of her and became absorbed in the details of the moving pictures she had taken. Once, he frowned.

'It's not edited yet, Jake. You shouldn't really see it until I——'

'Shh! Quiet and let me look at it.' She opened her mouth to retort, but closed it again. He wouldn't listen until he was done watching.

'It's going to be good,' he told her when the last of the tape had played. 'Very good.'

'I hoped it would,' she breathed, her eyes glowing with pleasure.

Sounds of music drifted in on the night air.

'Good taste in music,' Jake commented. 'Shall we go listen?'

Outside, they sat on the side deck, leaning against the cabin as they drank their tea and listened to the music across the water. The sun was setting, sending red streaks across the water. The ancient trees on shore had trans-

formed themselves into black silhouettes—the whole
world a painting in black and red from the sunset.

'Did you really talk to Marty?' Jake asked. The music
stopped briefly, then strains of the *Blue Danube* came
to them on the night air.

She drew her legs up, slipping her arms around them.
'I phoned him, but—I thought about selling it to him,
but I wouldn't really do that, Jake. I don't know what
I'll do.'

'I could market it for you,' he offered, adding swiftly,
'No, don't misunderstand me, Jenny. You keep copyright. I'll just act as your agent.'

'Why? What would you get out of that?'

She was eyeing him uneasily, but he said frankly, 'I'd
like you to work with me on this Queen Charlotte film.'

If she said yes, she'd be on location, working side by
side with Jake. She wanted badly to say yes, but she
evaded, 'You're going to do it?'

'If you'll help. I can't do it alone. I honestly don't
have the perspective. I love this place, but you know
what would happen if I tried to put together a film on
it.'

She nodded. 'You're too close to it. You wouldn't be
able to weed out the——'

'Drivel?' he suggested wryly.

She giggled. 'You're an artist. Artists don't produce
drivel.'

'Not even about hamburgers?'

'Well, that, maybe,' she agreed with a grin. 'How is
that last Madison film going?'

'Hans is doing it. At least—he'd better be doing it. If
not, he's getting his walking papers. Right now we could
spend some time——'

'Make notes?' she suggested, reading his mind. 'Do
research?' She shouldn't. She knew it was better to make
a clean break, but she found herself getting excited
against her will.

'Set up a story-board?' he suggested. 'You'd have to direct this one, Jenny.'

'Co-direct,' she amended. Could she get hold of a story-board pad in Queen Charlotte? Not a chance! Jake would have to send for one from Vancouver. Jake was watching, assessing her reaction. She challenged him, 'You know very well we'll be thrashing out every scene. You couldn't keep your fingers off it.'

'It worked well on the Swiftsure film, didn't it?' he asked softly, making Jenny feel breathless, as if they were talking about more than films.

'Yes, it did,' she agreed slowly. 'It was a great film.'

The pink had faded to darkness. A long-necked crane flew along the shoreline, a black silhouette against the sky.

'Will you do it, Jenny?'

She turned to look at him, trying to penetrate the darkness. She demanded softly, 'What are you asking of me, Jake?'

'Just this film.' His voice was impersonal and low in the darkness. 'Have your trip with George. We'll get together here and there along the way, work out the details. Then next spring you can fly back from the Caribbean—or wherever—and we can come up here for the filming.'

He must have sensed her silent weakening. He said, 'I'll take you around when we get back to Queen Charlotte. I'll show you the village. We'll get Luke to fly us to some of the old villages.'

'You've got to be in Keremeos in three days,' she reminded him. 'What's happening to the museum pamphlet? And that Heysworth film that was developing? Don't you have to get back to Vancouver?'

He ticked off each item on his fingers, a smile in his voice. 'The pamphlet is done, at the printers now. Charlotte is keeping track of it, and she'll call Violet with a message for me if there's any problem. The Heysworth contract is signed, but I got the dates put off. You and I have time to do some sightseeing—two days' worth before I have to catch the plane and get to work on Chris's mountain climbing. We'll take cameras, get some film—just to get a feel for it.' He was standing up, as if everything was settled.

She said nervously, 'You're trying to pressure me.'

'If I don't, you'll disappear on me.'

'Yes,' she whispered, admitting it, knowing it would be better if she did, if he didn't keep coming after her, making her realise how much she would miss him.

'I can't let you do that, Jenny.'

When he talked in that voice, there was no point arguing with him. He would have his way.

'All right,' she said slowly, unwillingly. 'We'll go. We'll look. But I'm not promising anything. It doesn't mean I'll say yes, Jake.'

He nodded, satisfied for the moment. 'All right. Right now you'd better show me around this vessel, then we'll get some sleep. We've got an early start tomorrow.'

She didn't expect to sleep well. She could hear Jake's sounds through the thin wall of her state-room, the sound of his clothes sliding off his body, the covers being pulled back as he got into bed. She breathed softly, quietly, and she could hear Jake breathing nearby.

She closed her eyes and listened. If she spoke, he would hear her. She knew from his breathing that he was not yet asleep. She listened, waiting for his breathing to deepen.

If she got up, walked into the cabin where he slept, he would take her in his arms and make love to her. She closed her eyes, wanting his touch, her body coming alive from the memory of his hands and his lips making love to her.

The door to his cabin was open. She would have heard if he had closed it. Was he asleep yet? What would he do if she did come to him?

She'd be standing in the corridor, looking in, trembling, afraid he wouldn't want her after all. Then, if he did, if he took her hand and drew her into his arms, she'd have the morning to face.

She slept poorly, waking several times, each time fighting the battle with herself, wanting to go to Jake, yet afraid.

She was up with the sun, washing and getting breakfast ready, managing to look as if she'd slept well instead of spending the night in frustrated longing.

It was natural enough, she supposed. She hadn't had a lover since Lance. She was a normal woman, having her woman's needs stirred for the first time in years.

She shook her head, admitting to herself that it was more than that. It wasn't just sex she wanted. It was Jake.

Jake was casual and businesslike as he ate breakfast, then got them underway. Jenny followed his instructions as he steered *Lady Harriet* through the channel. She held the chart, spotted markers, confirmed his estimates of their progress with detailed examinations of the chart while he fought the wild currents. Twice, they passed empty hulks of wrecked ships on the shore. Then they were through, approaching Queen Charlotte.

The floats were full, so Jake brought *Lady Harriet* in to raft against a fishing-boat. The skipper helped with the lines, staring at Jake and finally asking, 'You're Mary Hall's boy, aren't you?'

Boy? Jenny smiled, watching Jake and the fisherman deep in conversation as they tied the lines. Then, when the lines were tied to their satisfaction and the fishing talk was over, Jake led her off towards the town.

'Violet made me promise to bring you to dinner. Do you want to visit George first, to reassure her about the boat?'

'Yes, please, but I'm not dressed for dinner! I don't have any clothes with me for that sort of thing!'

'This is Queen Charlotte, not high society Vancouver. Violet's not going to care what you're wearing—she's a blue jeans lady herself, so you'll feel right at home.'

Jake's aunt was astonishingly beautiful, her long black hair framing a face that was proud and dramatically angular.

'Jenny, come in. I've been looking forward to meeting you. You certainly look better than you did when I saw you at the hospital.'

'You saw me at the hospital?'

'You were sleeping—sleeping off the clams, I guess.'

Violet and her husband Nat lived in a home that was set up on the hillside with a view of the harbour. Their living-room was gently littered with the signs of their wide interests—magazines ranging from *Time* and *Newsweek* to a West Coast fishing magazine. A rug-hooking project was spread out near a comfortable chair.

'Your design?' asked Jake, walking over to the partly finished rug which bore the outline of a large, black raven.

'Yes,' Violet agreed. 'I wanted to use it for the hallway, but Nat says it's sacrilege for us to walk on the sacred raven.' She laughed, drawing a smile from Jake. 'And how would he know? He's the white man.'

'Is Nat working late?' asked Jake, his warm voice revealing his affection for Violet's husband.

'No, he'll be here any minute. He doesn't often work late—it's Laurie who does most of the overtime. She's younger, and full of energy. Make yourself comfortable, Jenny. I've got coffee on—or are you full of coffee?'

'I'd love some. We left the coffee-pot on the stove when we went ashore the other day—it got so terribly burned that Jake and I are plotting throwing it overboard and buying George a new pot.'

'It didn't start a fire?'

'No,' Jake explained. 'It's one of those enclosed Dickenson stoves.'

Violet bestowed a smile on Jake, making Jenny realise that the older woman thought they were lovers. She glanced at Jake, but he seemed intent on examining a magazine that was lying open on a coffee table.

Jenny couldn't help feeling she was being swept along, given a part in a play over which she had no control. When they were alone together in the living-room, Jenny started to say, 'You and Monica——'

'We'll talk about Monica another time,' interrupted Jake swiftly.

He looked uncomfortable, even guilty. Just how honest had he been with Monica about his intentions—or lack of intentions?

What if she went back? Would Jake take her love and turn it into an award-winning film? She laughed bitterly, but couldn't tell him why when he asked.

Over dinner she watched Violet gently teasing her husband. Later, while they relaxed in the living-room listening to music, the pilot, Luke, arrived with his wife, Laurie.

Lovers. Jenny was surrounded by lovers. Luke's eyes never seemed to leave his vivacious, dark-haired wife. Laurie became involved in a heated discussion with Jake about media coverage of the recently publicised Haida land claims, but her eyes kept moving to her husband as if in a silent communication.

'I want to interview you, Jake, about this film you're thinking of doing,' said Laurie when she learned about it.

'It won't be started until next year,' Jake told her. 'But you should interview Jenny, not me. It's up to her whether we do it or not.'

'You are doing it, aren't you, Jenny?' Laurie twisted on the stool she was seated on, her lively eyes turning to Jenny. 'You've got to—it'll make a fabulous film! We'll do a series on it at the radio station. Everyone will be interested, because you're doing a film about us all.'

Jenny glared at Jake, resenting this kind of indirect pressure. She shrugged and said, 'Time will tell.'

Laurie glanced searchingly at them both, then changed the subject.

'I hope you do it,' said Luke suddenly. 'I don't get to hear Laurie on the air very often since she got promoted. I miss her voice when I'm flying.' Then he explained for Jenny's startled look, 'I've got a broadcast radio in the Beaver.'

Jenny couldn't help envying them the love they shared. Then, somehow, she got herself involved in a conversation with Laurie, speculating on the form a film about the island might take.

She glanced at Jake, and saw something like victory in his eyes. Getting Jenny planning the film was a big step towards victory.

The next day, Jake borrowed Violet's car and took her to the Haida village of Skidegate, where he showed her the inside of the band council building, a modern construction following the style of the old Haida longhouses. One end of the building—a wall of glass—faced the ocean.

'What a place to work!' breathed Jenny, seated in an office chair that looked straight out on to the ocean, listening to Jake talk with the band manager.

This wasn't at all what she had expected. These villagers were politically and socially aware. They knew the world outside their islands. Many of them made regular winter holiday trips to Hawaii. Yet, despite the way they adopted the white man's trappings with enthusiasm, they retained a beautiful individuality that showed in their art, their pride in their heritage.

Jake took her farther up the coast, stopped at Saint Mary's Spring where he urged her to drink the water, warning her, 'The legend says that if you drink the water, you'll always return to the islands.'

So she drank, for how could anyone visit these islands without dreaming of returning again some day?

'Tired?' he asked hours later as they drove along the highway back to Queen Charlotte.

'Yes,' she admitted. 'Walked out, talked out, exhausted.'

'I'll take you to the beach at Tlell. You can relax there.'

Miles of sandy beach. Another memory, she thought, shaking her head to clear a welling of tears as Jake took her hand and led her out on to the sand, to a big old log that made a perfect back rest for two tired people.

The surf swept in over the beach, repeating its pattern with hypnotic regularity. Jenny let herself lean back, hardly aware when her eyes drooped. Then Jake shifted and she came sharply awake.

'Sorry, I'm dropping off,' she said nervously, sitting up, watching him, wishing he would touch her, kiss her—and afraid that he would.

She was terrified that his probing eyes knew exactly what she was thinking. Then he said casually, 'Make yourself comfortable. Have a sleep, then I'll take you for dinner.'

He slipped his arm around her and she found her head resting against his shoulder, her eyes closing again.

She opened her eyes later and found Jake's face only inches away, his eyes closed. Was he sleeping? She lay very still, comfortable yet troubled. Jake shifted in his sleep, his other arm closing around her, drawing her closer.

She should pull away.

How was she ever going to overcome her love for him if she kept letting him get close to her like this? She was waking up every morning from dreams of Jake in her arms. She'd been planning her own career only days ago, a plan that didn't include him. Yet now she was becoming firmly entangled in his life, his plans for her.

George would be out of the hospital soon, then perhaps Jenny could get hold of herself, make plans that didn't include Jake.

Later, when he was gone back to Vancouver, she would talk sense into herself. But right now—right now she didn't want to.

She closed her eyes and gave herself up to the pleasure of his arms around her, drifting off to sleep herself.

When she woke, she found Jake's jacket rough under her cheek. She sat up, disorientated, brushing sand off her clothes, looking around and finding Jake's tall form outlined against the water as he stood at the edge, just above the tide line, looking out on a stormy sea.

He turned just as she stood up, walking towards her without speaking. She picked up his jacket from the sand, shaking it out and handing it to him.

'I must have slept a long time.'

His eyes followed the curve of her breasts under her shirt. He said absently, 'Not long. Are you hungry?'

'I don't know.' She pushed a nervous hand through her hair. 'I'm still half-asleep.'

'You'll be wanting food by the time you've woken up. Which would you prefer, Chinese or Canadian? There's only two choices in Queen Charlotte this time of day.'

'Chinese, I guess,' she decided, taking refuge in the details of small talk. 'Then I should have a look at your films. You must have taken miles of pictures today.'

'You can look it over later and see what you think— but not today. You need to sleep. We'll have dinner, then I'll take you back to *Lady Harriet*. Incidentally, why isn't it *Lady George*?'

She leaned against the car to brush her feet free of sand, then put her shoes on. 'It was already named when George and Scott bought it—George says it's bad luck to change a boat's name.'

'Lots of people do it. Come on, hop into the car. You're shivering. That jacket can't be very warm.'

As he had promised, Jake fed her and delivered her early to the boat so that she could get a good sleep.

She slept very poorly, however, lying awake, telling herself she was crazy to let Jake get her into this project; then admitting that—regardless of how crazy it was—she wanted to do it.

Would he be involved with another woman by the time they started filming? Or was he still seeing Monica, despite his intention not to marry her?

What if she made a play for Jake herself? He wanted her. He'd wanted her for a long time. She'd seen his eyes on her, but pretended not to notice, to care.

She smoothed her hands over her heated body, imagined they were Jake's hands. How many nights? How long before he tired of Jenny and turned away for someone else?

Her skin went cold and clammy, shuddering with the desperation of Jake's walking away, leaving her.

If he stayed much longer she would be lost. Much longer and her lips would open and the words would spill out, love words she knew better than to say to any man.

George might be out of hospital by the time Jake left. She'd developed a slight cough and the doctor was cautiously insisting she stay under his care until he was sure there were no ill effects from her bout with the clams.

Meanwhile, there was no excuse for Jenny not to go with Jake on his tour of the islands, and she admitted to herself that even if she had an excuse, she would probably be climbing into the Beaver the next morning, setting off for the abandoned villages to unearth overgrown totem poles and search for the ruins of old longhouses that had once been filled with living people.

They had a picnic lunch on Anthony Island, among ancient and restored totem poles. What a film this was going to make! Jake was running through tape at a furious rate, and she was taking pictures to remind herself of details rather than for any artistic purpose. Jake would do the filming on this production.

'Are we going to do it, Jenny?' he asked late in the afternoon, coming up behind her as she stared out at the water from the abandoned village site of Skedans.

'Yes, we'll do it,' she told him, not knowing when she had reached that decision. She didn't turn to look at him, but she heard him sigh. Having committed herself, she was suddenly frightened, wishing the words back.

She walked away from him, picking her way carefully down the hillside towards the waiting seaplane.

'Where now?' asked the pilot as they settled back into the Beaver. Today their pilot wasn't Luke, but one of the other pilots who worked for his charter company.

'Back to Queen Charlotte,' said Jake.

Their take-off was bumpy in the swell that was running in from Hecate Strait. Jake took her hand as they lifted, opening her clenched fingers.

'I'll be all right once we're up,' she insisted, but she left her hand in his. 'Just talk to me about something, would you?'

'What would you like?' He smiled, holding her gaze and making her forget they were airborne. 'History of the islands? I've been holding forth on that for the last two days. Did I tell you about the cows at city hall? Yes, of course. You were there at the time. What I'd really like is to tell you——' He broke off, a flush spreading over his face. Then he said ruefully, 'I guess I'll have to tell you about my unruly childhood.'

And he did, talking about his summers on fishing-boats, his apprenticeship to his grandfather, the carver. She had seen the children in the village, and she could picture him there, but beneath his words she heard more.

'You were a lonely child, too, weren't you, Jake?'

'I suppose I was,' he agreed, his eyes letting her see the child he had been. 'I didn't quite fit in anywhere. My father's people and my mother's were so much at odds with each other. I guess my parents were very deeply in love, but they died before I was old enough to know them very well.'

He shrugged, tightening his hand on hers. 'I had no real complaints. I certainly had all the creature comforts I could have wanted. In that way I suppose I was spoiled. I was a wild youngster, you know.'

Jenny laughed, her voice teasing, 'You're not so tame as a man, either.'

His breath caught and for a moment they were both silent, then he said huskily, 'Can I talk you into dinner? Please? Chinese again?'

He didn't want to leave her, she realised, her heart pounding. He was trying to stretch out their moments together.

Hesitantly, she offered, 'Why don't I cook for you? There are still salmon steaks in George's freezer.'

He didn't let himself show surprise, just said casually, 'Sounds good. I'll drop you off, then I'll go beg a bottle of wine from Violet and Nat.' He grinned boyishly. 'I'll wine you, and you can dine me.'

This had been her idea, but it was a dangerous one. Alone with Jake on the boat, anything could happen! She hesitated.

'Backing out, Jenny?' he asked softly, his mouth curved in a smile that didn't reach his eyes. 'We can still go Chinese if you like.'

She met his eyes. She knew the danger, but—no matter what the consequences, she needed his arms around her once more.

Her voice husky, she answered, 'No, Jake. I'm not backing out.'

CHAPTER TEN

'SMELLS good.'

Jenny swung around, still holding a dish filled with steaming scalloped potatoes. 'Jake! I didn't hear you come in.'

'Sorry.' He was smiling slightly, standing in the companionway, filling it with his breadth. 'You were humming—singing to yourself.'

'Yes. I heard this song on the radio—it's catchy. I—I like your sweater. It looks nice.' Luckily she was holding the bowl, or her hands might have followed their impulse to smooth the soft brown mohair of the sweater that he wore over smooth brown trousers.

'I'll tell Violet you approve—she gave it to me. She's an incurable knitter, you know.'

Jenny said breathlessly, 'I liked her.'

'She liked you.' Jake's voice wasn't very steady, either. 'She said that I—here, let me take that bowl for you.'

'I—no, it's hot! You'll burn yourself!'

He stepped back to let her pass. She put the bowl down on the table. He was watching her, a look in his eyes as if he were planning a film shot. She smoothed her hands nervously down over her slacks. At least she hadn't worn jeans, and her blouse was pretty, but——

'You're looking very beautiful, Jennifer.'

'I——' She felt so tongue-tied this evening, as if she were on her first date. She shouldn't be thinking that way, but she couldn't seem to help herself. When she'd invited him, she'd insanely intended to let him make love to her, but she'd regained her sanity and now she felt nervous and uncertain.

166

Jake lifted a hand as if to touch her, then dropped it, his voice husky as he offered, 'Can I set the table for you? No, that's all right, I'll find my way around. I was watching you put away the dishes the other night. I'll manage.'

They worked quietly together. When the salmon and potatoes were steaming on the table between them, and they were sitting across from each other, the silence seemed suddenly long and filled with meaning.

He was dressed more formally tonight, not unlike the way he dressed in the city. If she closed her eyes a little, let their surroundings blur, she could imagine they were seated at the small table in the breakfast nook she'd seen in his False Creek apartment.

Before she realised what she was going to say, she asked, 'Have you ever lived with anyone, Jake? A woman?'

He wanted to say no, but he couldn't tell her anything but the truth, so he said, 'Yes,' and saw her eyes drop away from his. He said quickly, 'But I didn't——'

'More potatoes?' she asked on a rush, following the serving of potatoes with a discussion of the Anthony Island restoration. Brightly, she asked, 'You'll want shots of Anthony Island? Those totem poles looking out to sea?'

'Of course,' he agreed, adding abruptly, 'Her name was Alison. It was six or seven years ago. We lived together for six months or so.'

Jenny said coldly, 'It doesn't matter.'

'I don't even remember what she looked like,' he added, realising as her eyes met his that he was only making it worse, painting himself into a corner as a man who never stuck to a woman. Alison, he thought bitterly. She'd been trouble from the beginning, a beautiful body with an empty head.

Jake gave up on explaining Alison, kept the conversation firmly on the details of filming. Eventually, to his relief, Jenny began to relax again.

'I'll get some paper to make notes,' she said at one point. He stopped her with a hand on her arm.

'Don't. We'll start planning next time. I've got to catch the jet tomorrow—there isn't time for us to really get into it. Does George's stereo work? How about some music?'

Jake had found George's collection of tapes, and was frowning over her cousin's taste. He wanted to take Jenny in his arms, love her, tell her all the words she wasn't ready to hear yet. Instead he forced himself to say casually, 'Country? Jazz? Not exactly what I had in mind—here's something!'

They listened to the strains of Ferrante and Teicher as they did the dishes. When Jenny had finished washing, she started to help Jake dry but he took her towel away, insisting, 'I'll finish the drying. You curl up on the settee and enjoy the music. You can watch me work.' He wanted to see her there, to watch her and pretend she was waiting for him to come to her.

'I thought you hated dishes?'

He shrugged and smiled, and she wasn't about to fight for the privilege of drying dishes, so she went into the salon. She tucked her feet up, leaned back on a soft cushion. Then she closed her eyes, listening to the music, but whenever she opened them, Jake was there, close by.

In her mind, the dreams started again. She couldn't seem to stop them. She found herself waiting for the moment when he came to her.

When he sat down near her, she watched him from behind lowered lids, taking pleasure in the sight of him relaxed and still only inches away from her.

They talked—meaningless, comfortable spurts of conversation.

'Your plane leaves in the morning,' she said at one point, meeting his eyes with uncharacteristic challenge. 'Shouldn't you spend the evening with your aunt? You haven't seen her in a long time and——'

'I'd rather be here,' he said hoarsely, as she had hoped he would. Then he looked at her oddly and said, 'Jennifer? Jenny?'

She fell silent, staring at him, frightened by the sudden intensity of his eyes.

'What? What is it, Jake?'

He started to say something, stopped, shook his head, started again. 'Jenny, I honestly don't know how to deal with you any more. Damn,' he said softly, smiling wryly, 'I'm not used to feeling so helpless. You were always there, and I know I took you for granted, but now, suddenly, you're so—I'm afraid if I say the wrong thing, you'll disappear on me again. I'm not sure what you want, and I——'

She felt an overwhelming urge to cry. She wanted to touch his face, smooth that disturbing look away, give him whatever it was that he wanted.

'What is it that you want of me?' she asked on a frightened whisper.

'You know what I want.' His arm lifted, his hand touching hers, fingers running up along her arm, touching her neck lightly, tracing the planes of her face.

Her lips parted, her breathing shallow. He was closer, both hands feeling the contours of her face, fingers spreading through her short hair as her scalp tingled with his touch.

His voice was low and hoarse. 'My God! I'm sure the whole world knows what it is I want of you by this time!'

His lips brushed hers. Was it his mouth trembling? Or hers? She drew in a deep, ragged breath. His head blotted out the red sky she had glimpsed through the porthole.

At first his mouth was soft and cautious against hers, then his hands tightened on her shoulders, his mouth became firm and warm, and her eyes closed to shut out everything but the wonderful feeling of Jake holding her, touching her, kissing her, drawing his tongue along her lip, exploring her cheek, her neck, the sensitive hollow of her throat with his mouth.

'Jennifer——' He drew her soft body close against his, sliding his arm around her back and bringing her close. She found her arms around his shoulders, her palms open on his back, stroking the soft mohair, feeling the ridges of his shoulder muscles tense as her hands moved. She felt the fire rising swiftly in her blood, her hands rubbing against his hard male body, his gasp as her hand moved against him.

'Jennifer—Jenny——'

'Jennifer,' she told him softly, her breast swelling from nothing more than the thought of his touch on it. 'You can call me Jennifer if you want.'

'You said you didn't like it.' He hardly knew what he was saying. His hands were exploring the back of her ribcage, tracing her spine through the thin blouse she wore.

She opened her eyes and stared into the black depths of his. She felt dizzy, heat racing through her veins. 'I've missed you calling me Jennifer—I——' His fingers moved softly along her side, skirting the swelling of her breast, not quite touching the softness that swelled suddenly, aching for his caress.

'Please, Jake,' she whispered, her eyes refusing to stay open, her hands clutching, digging into his back. Then his lips were on hers again, hard and suddenly demanding. She was opening her lips, herself to him, spinning off, losing touch with everything except the reality of Jake's lips, Jake's tongue, Jake's hands cupping the fullness of her breasts.

'Jennifer—oh, God! Darling ...' His lips pulled a response from hers that she had never known existed. She was burning, needing him, moving against him to feel his warmth closer to her, hardly hearing his words as his hot breath stirred against her ear and her throat. 'I've needed you for so long, darling! Let me love you!'

Her fingers slid under the edge of his sweater, found the dry warmth, the sudden rigidity of his abdominal muscles as she moved her palms against him, up to his broad, hard chest.

He stared at her, her eyes closed, head thrown back to expose her soft throat for his kiss. He touched the vulnerable skin with his lips, seeing her shudder as his lips traced along the softness, down to the beautiful swelling of her woman's breast. He kissed the peak softly, then caressed it with his tongue, feeling the powerful surge of his own desire as she groaned and twisted against him.

He should make sure she knew what she was doing, that the morning wouldn't leave her regretting this intimacy. He moved his hand along her midriff, caressing through the soft fabric of her slacks, feeling her respond to his touch, needing him.

He wanted her for ever, her soft body lying against his. His lips moved over the white skin, seeking all the places that would drive her wild in his arms, wanting to touch and kiss and love, wishing suddenly that he could give her his child, could touch her and hold her and love her and make her his more deeply than any two people had ever joined.

He lifted her, holding her against his chest, touching her lips again before he moved along the passageway, carrying her held closely in his arms. She closed her eyes, sliding one arm around his shoulder. Her other palm explored the line of his clenched jaw.

Then she was resting against the softness of a mattress. She opened her eyes, staring up at him, seeing the movement of his chest that revealed shallow, ragged breathing.

He wanted her so badly. It was in his eyes, in the way he leaned over her, so still, so tense. Had he wanted her like this before? Or was it the evening, the islands, and George's music?

She loved him so much. She had always loved him, but now it had grown to an unbearable pain. She opened her lips to tell him, but his mouth covered hers and she was caught up in his kiss, trembling as his hands fumbled with the fastening of her slacks, finding her own hands working with the buttons of his shirt.

As the last vestige of her clothing disappeared, Jake's hand moved softly along the curve of her hip, his eyes looking down at her body with a sudden stillness.

She knew with a sharp pain that she was never going to recover from this night, never going to stop needing him. She hadn't been with a man since Lance, and she was fiercely, agonisingly glad that she was unprepared for this, that her surrender to him could mean the creation of a child in her womb.

'Jake,' she whispered, her hand caressing up along his chest, touching his face. She dared not whisper that she loved him. Instead, she said his name again.

'Jennifer ...' He brought his lips to hers again, taking her heated body in his arms.

She lost track of everything but the feel of him, the closeness of him. His lips and his hands caressed her, sending flames along her veins. Her hands answered his, touching him as she had never touched a man before.

When she couldn't bear the waiting any longer, needing him to possess her completely, she groaned, 'Please, Jake,' not even knowing she spoke, but responding eagerly and completely to his masculine possession of her body.

He took her to the edge of the world. She was mad with needing him, holding him, kissing him, sharing the motion of their two bodies becoming one. Then their passion climaxed in an explosive surge, and they lay trembling in each other's arms.

Finally, they slept, exhausted.

Once, in the night, Jenny awoke, opening her eyes and seeing the dark silhouette of Jake's form. His arms tightened around her. She closed her eyes, relaxing against his body, wanting the night to last for ever, trying not to think about what came next.

Held tightly against Jake, she slept again. She was curled against him when he woke in the early hours of the day. The northern sun was climbing in the sky, working its way into the cabin where they lay together.

She shifted, turning her face against him as the light intruded into her dream. Careful not to disturb her, he reached up and pulled the curtain down over the porthole. The cabin darkened.

He should wake her, but he didn't know what words to say when her eyes stared into his. He was afraid to say too much, afraid that she would waken regretting giving herself to him the night before.

Had it been too soon?

God! What if her eyes froze, shutting him out for ever? He couldn't face that.

He held her in his arms without waking her until the sun had risen high in the sky. He'd give her time to get used to the idea of him as a lover. Then, when he came back in a few days he would tell her all the words that had trembled on his lips last night.

She knew. After last night, she couldn't help knowing how he felt about her, how necessary she was to his happiness.

He brushed the short curls gently back from her face, pressed the softest of kisses on to her lips, and left her sleeping.

She was alone when she woke, lying in George's big double berth with the blankets tumbled around her. Her eyes opened slowly as she remembered. Jake. His hands and his lips giving pleasure to every part of her body.

He had taught her more about passion than she had ever known before. Her hands had explored the hard male contours of him, touching him in ways she had never thought to touch a man, discovering the pleasure of drawing a groan of desire from him, learning how the touch of her softness against him could arouse his need—and hers—when only a moment before they had lain spent in each other's arms.

The curtain was drawn, the light coming around the edges and filtering through the cabin. Jenny looked down along the length of her own body, her bare skin exposed and gleaming in the half-light.

Would there be a child from their union? She closed her eyes, feeling the fierce heat of Jake's touch. It was possible. She'd been totally unprepared for intimacy with a man, although Jake probably assumed that she was in the habit of taking lovers.

What if she were pregnant?

A baby would be hers. Jake wouldn't have to know. Not if she disappeared before it became obvious. She'd probably have to leave the west coast entirely to get away from Jake. How long would their affair last? A shaft of pain penetrated her as she thought about the inevitable ending. Would she have the strength to run away, leave before he tired of her?

Jake. He was gone. She felt the emptiness of the boat, listened to sounds from outside—the roar of an engine as a boat pulled away, the muted sound of voices on the wharf.

She stumbled as she got up, putting on her clothes quickly, seeing the clock and knowing when she heard the roar of a jet overhead that it was Jake—leaving her.

The note was lying on the galley counter. She saw it, her heart pounding, afraid to walk the two steps and read his black handwriting.

If he had wanted to tell her that he loved her, he could have said it last night when she was in his arms, closer than two people had ever been.

> Jennifer,
> I couldn't bear to wake you and say goodbye. I'll be back on Sunday.
>
>   Jake.

Not love, Just 'Jake'. And he'd left her alone. Of course she had known it would happen, but——

The note crumpled in her hand. There were chores to do, little household—or boathold—duties that might help her to take her mind off Jake.

At least she hadn't told him that she loved him.

He knew how badly she wanted him, but there was just a slight possibility that he didn't know it was love. Or had she said the words, some time in the night when his hands and his body were drawing everything she had into their union?

She must have. She couldn't have kept the words back, not when he touched her like that, when her need was surging through her veins, making her wild and reckless, foolishly fearless.

The boat moved under her feet gently. Someone had stepped on to the deck from the wharf. Jenny's heart pounded for a moment, then slowed with a sickening thud. Not Jake. Jake's step was heavier.

'Jenny?'

It was George's voice, George almost running across the deck and down the stairs. Jenny swung around to face her.

George looked slightly pale, but she was smiling, her eyes gleaming with her customary energy. She took in everything at a glance—the crumpled paper in Jenny's hand, the tumbled bedclothes through the doorway in her own cabin. Jenny watched her eyes dart from the bed and back to Jenny's face, watching George putting it all together.

'Where's Jake?'

Jenny shook her head, dropping the paper into the waste-paper basket beside her. George glanced at it, her hand moving in a brief spasm as if she wanted to pick it up and read it.

'He's gone,' Jenny said flatly, her voice almost normal. 'He took the plane south. Did the doctor let you out of the hospital?'

'I'm here, aren't I? As good as new, but with a healthy respect for clams!' George's voice dropped with concern. 'Are you all right, Jenny?'

Jenny turned away, said tightly, 'I didn't get any shopping done. We should go up to the store later and lay in stores, shouldn't we?'

'Jenny? What did you and Jake——'

'Could we just get out of here, George? I don't want to talk about it. He'll be back, but I can't see him. I just can't! I know you're still weak, but if we could just get our groceries and get the hell away from this place?'

George dropped her sweater on the dinette table. 'I'll have a coffee. We've got some artificial sweetener, don't we? There wasn't any in the hospital. Coffee tasted terrible!'

'You could have taken sugar in it.' Jenny managed a smile. 'You're such a little thing. I can't imagine a spoonful of sugar making you fat!'

'It won't if I don't have it.' George clicked a pill into her cup. 'Are you sure you want to go? Where?'

'I don't know. Anywhere. Just away from here.'

Jenny almost wondered if George wasn't deliberately dragging her heels. First they had to get groceries, then fuel, although *Lady Harriet*'s tanks were almost full. Then George wanted to wait another day because the stores were out of milk until the ferry arrived the next day.

The following day they left, but only after George had
made yet another trip up to the town for some last-minute
groceries she'd forgotten.

'We should have said goodbye to Violet,' George said
as they sailed past the town. 'She visited me in the hospital several times. Did you see the sweater I was wearing
when I came back from the hospital? She gave it to me.
She couldn't have knitted it in the last few days. I suppose
it was something she'd done for someone else, but it's
beautiful.'

Jenny looked up at the house where Violet and Nat
lived. She would have liked to have said goodbye, but
somehow she couldn't. Violet would look at her and see
too much. And then she might telephone Jake.

If he came back now——

She needed time before she could face him again.

They sailed *Lady Harriet* out around the sand bar.
The winds were from the south, not inviting for a passage
south to Vancouver Island. They worked their way slowly
south along the east coast of Moresby Island. So many
of the anchorages they stopped at were places she had
visited with Jake in the seaplane.

What a strange contrast travel was in this wilderness!
By boat they moved so slowly from place to place. With
the seaplane, she and Jake had hopped over the islands.
Roads were the normal method of travel to her mind,
but here there were only occasional, twisted logging roads
leading inland to stands of timber.

She would feel better when she got away from these
islands. They were too deeply steeped with memories of
Jake.

'Not tomorrow,' protested George when Jenny
suggested they cross to the mainland as soon as possible.
'We've been rushing down this coast. I'm tired, and I'm
not ready to cross the Hecate Strait yet.'

Jenny was startled. 'You're not afraid, George? I
didn't think you were afraid of anything.'

'Just a bit tired. Let's go back to the hot spring tomorrow.'

Jenny shrugged, knowing she was only fooling herself in thinking it would make a difference to get away from these islands.

Jake accused her of always running away, hiding herself. And she was doing it again, wasn't she? She loved him, yet making love with him had her running again, terrified.

No matter how many miles and days separated her from Jake, he would still be the owner of her heart. She'd spent enough days on this lonely sea to know that life held no excitement to match the times when he was near. She had hoped to find herself pregnant with his child, and that was still a possibility, but she knew now that it wasn't enough. Her life would be empty if she couldn't share it with Jake.

The thought terrified her, but she knew she had to go back to Vancouver, back to Jake. First she had to get control of herself, then she would go back and make herself so indispensable to him in every way that it would be Jenny—for ever.

None of his other women had been the one he would choose to have working at his side every day. That gave her an edge, and she had to try to fight for him. This wasn't anything at all like the love she had felt for Lance. When she closed her eyes, she couldn't even see Lance's face. Jake's would be engraved in her mind for ever.

Crossing to Hotspring Island, Jenny stood on deck, the wind made by their motion lifting her hair and causing her to button her jacket tightly.

A large sailboat passed, heading out into the strait. From the boats they had seen passing in the last two days, it seemed this was a popular place for departing on the long crossing to the mainland.

A seaplane flew past overhead, dropping down low. It wasn't unusual for passing planes to come down for a closer look—from curiosity, Jenny supposed.

The plane gained altitude after it passed them. Jenny looked back, watching the silver body reflect sunlight.

Was it turning? Coming back this way? It had flown east, as if towards the mainland, but now it seemed closer. With the wind of their motion in her ears, Jenny couldn't hear any other sounds. She stared, her heart thundering loud as *Lady Harriet*'s engines seemed to fall silent.

The plane swept down, low and fast, then skimmed the water and settled back in its own wake in mid-channel.

If the plane was going to Hotspring Island, it had stopped a mile short of its destination.

George had cut the engine right back. The boat was slipping along slowly. 'George, what have you——'

'I left a message for him,' confessed George, not meeting Jenny's eyes.

'Oh, lord!' She felt her flaming cheeks with her hands. She wasn't ready, not yet. She groaned, 'I'm going to make a terrible fool of myself.'

The plane's engine roared. Jenny swung around to see it taxiing slowly towards them, then turning to move parallel with *Lady Harriet*, matching their speed.

The passenger door opened and Jake stepped out on to the pontoon.

'What do you want me to do?' George shouted across to Jake.

His eyes on Jenny, Jake called back, 'Just cut the engine. We'll come up to you!'

With *Lady Harriet*'s engine silent, there was only the muted sound of the idling seaplane engine. Jake, standing only feet away on the pontoon of the plane, was hanging on to a strut with one hand.

She wasn't ready for this! It was too soon! She wanted to run into his arms, swim to him if she had to, but she was too frightened to move. She'd planned to come back on her own terms, make herself indispensable to him, but she knew with sick conviction that it wouldn't work. He wanted her now. Lance had once wanted her too, but only as a lover.

It wouldn't last.

He was staring at her, waiting for some sign. Why had he come? Oh, God! It was too soon and she was terrified!

Desperate, frightened, she shouted, 'Jake, I'm not going to do that film!' Her voice carried loud across the water to him. 'I won't do the Charlottes film—or any film!'

Oh, lord! What was she doing? What was she saying? What if he left, stepped back into the plane and never came back? She whispered, 'Jake, don't go,' but of course he didn't hear.

He was shouting back at her, his voice oddly hoarse, but she couldn't hear for the pounding in her ears.

Jake reached out and caught the rope George must have thrown. Then Luke was with him on the pontoon and Jake, suddenly, was on the deck, coming closer.

She wanted to run flying into his arms. Her hands clenched, her fingernails biting into her palms. His face was hard and lined, his dark, angry eyes glaring at her.

Weakly, she said, 'You're supposed to be in Keremeos.'

'Am I?' He stopped. For a scary, wonderful moment, she thought he was going to kiss her. Then his hands were deep in his pockets and he was pacing, prowling as if he were afraid to come near her.

'Jake, I—I'm afraid I can't——' She fell silent. There was nothing she could say, except that she loved him. She was terrified, not knowing what he really wanted from her—an affair? A one-night stand?

He was standing with his legs aggressively apart, but his face was pale and uncertain, his voice husky. 'It doesn't matter, Jenny.'

What didn't matter? The film? Her?

He said slowly, emphasising every word, his voice growing to a shout, 'You don't have to do the film. I don't give a damn about the film!'

The deck shifted underfoot and Jenny grabbed hold of the lashed mainsail to steady herself.

Her heart was thundering with a sick mixture of hope and fear that she somehow managed to keep out of her voice. 'Then why are you here? What is it you want from me—Jake, are you all right? Are you catching 'flu?'

He choked, '*Catching*—damn it, Jennifer! I——' He swung away, staring briefly at the waiting seaplane, at George standing nearby in the cockpit. Then his eyes were probing hers again. 'Jennifer—Jenny, do whatever you want, but——'

His voice broke off, came back in a strangled choke, 'Just—please don't leave me, Jennifer!' He lifted his arm to brush at his eyes where she could see tears glistening. 'Anything else—I can take anything else, but...don't run away from me. If you don't want to work with me, I can accept that,' he said in a strange, cold voice, then his eyes grew hot and his voice hoarse as he confessed, 'but I can't take it if you walk away from me again! When you walked out on me, Jenny, my whole world fell apart.'

She could see it in his face, the pain and the loss, the need that he'd never let her see before. Not only sexual need, but more, deeper than words could go.

'Jake,' she whispered, she had to understand, 'why did you say you were going to marry Monica?'

'Damn Monica!' His hands jerked out of his pockets, spread in a helpless gesture. 'I—hell! You asked, and I had this insane, irrational thought that you'd care. I

was—I was hoping to get a reaction out of you! Jenny.
If I marry anybody——'

'A reaction,' she repeated. He'd got a reaction; he'd
sent her world upside down and Jenny herself running.

'Jenny,' he pleaded, touching her with a hesitant hand.
'Did you care at all?'

She opened her mouth on a denial, but the need and
pain in his face was confusing her. She found herself
confessing, 'I couldn't stay and watch you with her. I
kept telling myself that your women didn't matter, that
they were just a meaningless series—I told myself I didn't
want to be one of them, but I——'

She started to tell him she couldn't stand thinking
about the day when he would leave her, but the tears
were welling up. She gulped and Jake grabbed her
shoulders, hard, groaning, 'Jennifer, you're the only one
who's ever gotten under my skin. Ever since you came,
I've wanted you. I didn't know how badly you'd gotten
to me until you tried to walk away, but I knew you'd
messed me up for any other woman.' His hands were
tracing her face, stroking the tension from her as he confessed hoarsely, 'I kept trying, because you didn't seem
to want me and—*damn* it, Jenny! Most of the time I
couldn't even—er—perform when it came down to it!
Monica!' He made an angry, frustrated noise that
couldn't have been a laugh. 'You thought we were lovers,
but we weren't—how the bloody hell could I make love
to a woman with your face in my mind all the time? Will
you please stop staring at me like that and *say*
something?'

She wasn't sure she could talk. Her knees were
shaking, her throat dry. 'What do you want me to say?'

He gave an exasperated, half-angry laugh. 'I've been
flying around for the last two days, searching for you
and this damned boat.'

He loved her. He hadn't actually said so, but his face
and his eyes told her. She had to tell him it was all right,

but the words were so difficult to say. 'What brought you back?' she asked instead.

'I was up in the mountains with Chris, but—I got scared! Damn, ever since—— I spend my life terrified you'll disappear, that I'll mess it up and lose you! That night, together on this boat, I thought—I knew you weren't ready for me to tell you I loved you—I was terrified that you'd wake up sorry. Jennifer, I'm not used to this—being in love, feeling so damned scared, terrified you'll tell me to go to hell! Except, sometimes— maybe I'm crazy, but sometimes I think that you love me, too—if you'd only admit it. I—will you at least say you're glad to see me?'

Her throat was filled with a large lump. Her heart was pounding hard, making her ears ring. His whole body was filled with tension, the pallor of his face a pale shadow of the Jake she knew.

'Jenny, for God's sake don't go silent and mysterious on me again! The night I made love to you, I kept hoping there would be a child.' He groaned out a confession, 'God help me, I don't know which I wanted most, your child—or the knowledge that a child might keep you with me. I can't—— Tell me what you're thinking!'

'I'm glad to see you,' she whispered, 'and I wanted there to be a baby, too.' Then she got her arms moving, wrapped tightly around his neck, her face buried in the soft mohair of his sweater.

'Will you please look at me?' he growled.

She could feel him trembling under her touch. She tipped her head back and met his eyes, trying to take in his need, his fears. 'I'm scared,' she whispered, then opened her lips for his deep, searing kiss.

It seemed an eternity before he whispered back, 'I've been scared ever since you walked into my studio five years ago. I kept trying to tell myself it was only sex, but I knew damned well—— I went through such a string of women, trying to tell myself I couldn't possibly be hopelessly in love with a woman who wouldn't even let me take her to dinner!'

'I kept wishing I could dare to say yes when you asked me out,' she admitted tremulously, 'but I was too much of a coward.'

He growled, 'And I had no idea. We've lost so much time! Darling, when you went away—I knew I had to get you back somehow. I didn't admit to myself that I loved you until I was rushing you to hospital after that damned Red Tide! Then I thought I was losing you and it damned near killed me!'

She put her hands on his chest, feeling his muscles quiver as her fingers moved. 'Jake, about the film——'

He grasped her hands, slipped them around his waist and caught her close to him. He kissed her lips lightly, his voice deep and low. 'Darling, do whatever you have to do. I want you working with me. You know that. But please, Jennifer, please don't leave me. The rest doesn't matter.' His voice trembled to a whisper. 'When you go away, there's no light left, no joy. I need you, darling. I love you so much!'

'I love you,' she whispered back. 'I've always loved you.'

Luke called from the seaplane, 'Jake?'

'What does he want?' Jenny asked, but Jake's lips covered hers and for long moments there was nothing but the feel of his arms around her, the spinning ecstasy of his mouth taking hers.

Slowly, when he stopped kissing her, she realised that the roaring in her ears was not only from Jake's nearness.

'He's going?'

'Yes. And George.'

'George? But how—how could she——'

'She's leaving us alone, darling. She'll meet us in a few days, on Vancouver Island.'

She stiffened, remembering all George's trips into Queen Charlotte before they left. 'When did you set this up?'

His hands travelled down the length of her back, cupped her buttocks as he drew her close in a contact that had them both gasping as he asked, 'Do you mind?'

'No,' she breathed, twisting her fingers into his hair and pulling his mouth down to hers. 'But tell me.'

His tongue traced the outline of her lips, his eyelids drooping with desire as he watched her reaction to his touch. 'You taste wonderful,' he groaned.

'George?' she asked, her fingers caressing his neck, slipping down to fumble with his shirt buttons under the sweater.

'She called me,' he gasped. 'If you touch me like that, you'll never get the story!'

'What's the matter?' she whispered, her fingers pushing his shirt aside, returning to explore the muscular swelling of his spare male breast. 'Can't take it?' she taunted.

'I can take it,' he groaned, finding the edge of her sweater and running his hands up in a light caress that found every sensitive spot on her back, then around, along her ribcage, to the swellings of her breasts. Her fingers stilled when he found her nipples.

When she sagged, he grabbed her close with one strong arm, supporting her against him. 'Can't take it?' he asked softly, finally getting the sweater out of his way and lowering his lips to where his fingers had been. 'Jenny,' he groaned, his lips closing over her breast, 'I've needed you so badly.'

He straightened, trembling, drawing her against him. 'God, Jenny, I'm like a teenager! I can't wait. George— George called and said you were setting sail from Queen Charlotte, that she was going to keep you on the islands for as long as she could before you crossed to the mainland—I——' He gripped her tightly, covering her face with kisses again as he explained gruffly, 'She gave a list of anchorages you might be found in—and...I came as soon as I could. Do you know Sandspit airport has been fogged in for two days?'

She shook her head, touching his face, marvelling at the way the lines were smoothed, at the love that she saw shining from his eyes.

'Do you think we made a baby, Jake?'

'You——' He swallowed. 'Aren't you—aren't you on the Pill or something?'

She shook her head, admitted, 'There hasn't been anyone I've wanted to—there wasn't any reason to take the Pill.'

His hands were trembling as they dropped down to her shoulders, drew her close and caressed down the length of her back. 'Oh, God, Jenny! I thought—with Wayne, and all those men you dated—I went through agonies, imagining you and——'

She stopped his words with her lips. 'Jake, I love you,' she told him, her hands touching his face, her voice growing strong with confidence as she saw how much he wanted to hear those words again. Her hands explored his back, feeling the strong knot of muscles under her fingers.

He cupped her face with his hands and bent to brush a light kiss on her lips. Her arms tightened, drawing him closer as he pressed the long length of his body against hers, invading her softness, making her gasp, then groan before he lifted his head, looked around and said softly, 'We're alone—staying nicely in the middle of the channel.'

She laughed softly. 'I should hope we're alone. You've just stripped half my clothes off!'

'I've been waiting a long time,' he explained. 'You have to make allowances. I called Luke and booked his plane—and him as pilot. I told him that I'd appreciate

it if he flew me on this charter himself. That I might be
making a fool of myself, and I'd rather do it in front
of him than some stranger. He said he had a note waiting
for me, from George.'

'What did the note say?'

He didn't answer for a long moment. He was too busy
kissing and touching his love. 'She told me not to come
unless I was really in love with you.'

He had come. She pressed her cheek against his chest,
felt the thunder of his heart, the rumble of his voice
saying, 'When we landed, Luke told me this was a good
place for love—he fell in love with Laurie on that island
over there. You are going to marry me, aren't you,
Jennifer?'

He closed his eyes briefly, opened them again and
stated, 'If you say no, I'm afraid I'm going to keep after
you until you change your mind. I know I said you could
do whatever you had to if it didn't mean you left me,
but—it's got to be marriage, Jenny.' His hands slipped
down along her sides. He watched her eyes widen and
her lips part as he moved slowly closer. His own breath
was rough as he said, 'If you're not ready, I think there's
a chance I could change your mind—given time.'

'How?' she managed to ask on a gasp.

He was starting to smile again now, his eyes gleaming.
'Are you going to marry me? If you say no, would it
help if I held out on you, wouldn't kiss you until——
Oh, lord, Jenny, I can't even joke about that! You are
going to marry me, aren't you? You've got to!'

'Of course I am—though I shouldn't. You're doing it
again, you know. Steamrollering me. Only this time,
you've got George in on it.'

She could feel the laughter bubbling up, and the tears.
He had been hers, in her heart, for so long. Now she
would love him openly. To live with him and work with
him and love him. She was frightened by her own vulnerability, but she wasn't going to let it stop her from

loving Jake. Even one day with him was worth any of the lonely times that might follow.

'Marry me,' he growled, bending over her with a light in his eyes that made her shiver deliciously. 'Marry me first, then we can fight it out. I've never felt like this about anyone, Jenny.'

'You want me to marry you right away?' She smoothed her palms over his muscular chest, whispered, 'Isn't there anything you'd like to do first? After all, we're days away from a wedding licence.'

He pulled her closer as he looked around at the ocean and the islands. 'Let's have part of the honeymoon first,' he suggested, bending down to take possession of her lips. 'I'd like another try at making that baby of ours.'

She found herself laughing, moulding her body against his in a promise that he couldn't mistake. 'What if it doesn't work?' she asked on a gasp as his hands slipped down over her buttocks and pulled her close against him.

'Then we'll just have to try again,' he growled, silencing her laughter with his love.

The small yacht drifted slowly into the channel. Overhead, a raven swooped across the sky, looking down on the lovers.

The Perfect Gift.

Four new exciting novels from Mills and Boon:

SOME SORT OF SPELL – by Frances Roding
– An enchantment that couldn't last or could it?

MISTRESS OF PILLATORO – by Emma Darcy
– The spectacular setting for an unexpected romance.

STRICTLY BUSINESS – by Leigh Michaels
– highlights the shifting relationship between friends.

A GENTLE AWAKENING – by Betty Neels
– demonstrates the truth of the old adage 'the way to a man's heart…'

Make Mother's Day special with this perfect gift.
Available February 1988. Price: £4.80

YOU'RE INVITED TO ACCEPT **FOUR ROMANCES** AND A TOTE BAG **FREE!**

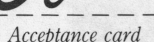

Acceptance card

NO STAMP NEEDED	Post to: Reader Service, FREEPOST, P.O. Box 236, Croydon, Surrey. CR9 9EL

Please note readers in Southern Africa write to:
Independant Book Services P.T.Y., Postbag X3010, Randburg 2125, S. Africa

YES! Please send me 4 free Mills & Boon Romances and my free tote bag – and reserve a Reader Service Subscription for me. If I decide to subscribe I shall receive 6 new Romances every month as soon as they come off the presses for £7.20 together with a FREE monthly newsletter including information on top authors and special offers, exclusively for Reader Service subscribers. There are no postage and packing charges, and I understand I may cancel or suspend my subscription at any time. If I decide not to subscribe I shall write to you within 10 days. Even if I decide not to subscribe the 4 free novels and the tote bag are mine to keep forever. I am over 18 years of age   EP20R

NAME _____
                                                              (CAPITALS PLEASE)

ADDRESS _____

_____

_____ **POSTCODE** _____

The right is reserved to refuse application and change the terms of this offer. You may be mailed with other offers as a result of this application. Offer expires March 31st 1988 and is limited to one per household.
Offer applies in UK and Eire only. Overseas send for details.